Home

(A Novel)

Heather Morrison

For Wee Nell

CHAPTER ONE

Maybeth opened the door to the Old Chandlery guest rooms and was immediately transported back to a time of ships clerks, boat building, bustle and raw rope. She had chosen to stay here for the duration of the contract. Her usual life was played out in the city of London. A world away from where she found herself now.

She was working for a large property firm who had small sub-offices all over the world. There was one here in the East Coast of Scotland. Her firm had been given this small property by the harbour in a small seaside village to sell and with life being what it was at the moment the peaceful shore-side retirement business was a very lucrative business to be in indeed.

Maybeth put her luggage on the floor and looked around the compact apartment. It had a living room/ bedroom combi, a small kitchen, and a bathroom with a shower. 'Ideal,' she thought. It didn't take much to please her. As long as there was wi-fi and a fridge for her wine she was happy. She sat on the bed and removed her shoes. Black, stiletto-heeled and Italian designer. All pre-requisite for the company, along with the bright red Porsche which now sat like a sore thumb outside her lodgings courtesy of Lawson & James property. The company had been set up in 1964 by Archie Lawson and Kenneth James. They had both now retired but Kenneth James had a daughter, Laura, who had taken the reigns of the business and made it one of the best performing and successful companies in the world. She really knew her stuff and was both ruthless and fair in equal measure. Maybeth had started with the company on a school work experience and was given an apprenticeship where she worked her way up. Laura and Maybeth got on well and she was a reliable and professional employee.

This Old Chandlery still had the old ships ropes, a bell and an ancient ships wheel embedded into walls that had been taken back to the bare brick of the 1800's when the building had been built. Maybeth let her imagination wander to a time when the bed she now sat upon was a wooden chair behind a polished oak desk where a clerk was sitting, pen in inkwell, taking down orders for shipping equipment – a new mast head or a wooden rudder perhaps. Her thoughts returned to the present and she walked over to the window. It looked directly onto the harbour where boats and dinghies bobbed up and down on the light waves. She was going to enjoy this job. She was here to sell a property and she was going to sell it, but hopefully not too quickly. She wanted a day or two to look around. She hadn't been to this part of Scotland for a very long time. There was more to this coastal village than a property to sell. This was where Maybeth's birth mother had lived. This was where Maybeth had been left outside the church manse in 1993. Minutes old they said, well wrapped up in knitted clothes with a 'please care for my baby, she is called Maybeth' tag wrapped around her tiny pink wrist. The ministers wife had found her and taken her inside. She had called the appropriate authorities. They had taken her into the City and she had been put up for adoption. She had been adopted quickly by a lovely couple who had moved her down South and given her everything she needed. Even love, which she knew through some of her friends who had also been through the adoption system was not always a given. Maybeth's parents had kept her name as it was unusual and they had liked it. They were also moving so far away that they doubted that anyone would try to find her and try and take her back. Not that should have been a worry either because once adopted, birth parents lost all rights to the child.

Maybeth was nervous and excited about being here. She did plan to dig a bit but needed to meet with Mark Vaughan who was heading up the company office here and the contact for the property. She decided to take a quick shower and go for a walk along the harbourside to the lido and then get a takeaway and a glass of wine before heading to bed early. It had been a long drive. She had been up since four a.m. It was just after eight in the evening and Mark Vaughan had made it very clear he liked a sunrise meeting. Seven thirty at his office on the West Point of the harbour. Maybeth moved away from the window and headed to the bathroom.

Pittenweem   October 1993

CHAPTER TWO

Avril sat in the cold alleyway with a biting wind hurling around her ears. She was hunched as low as she could get. She was scared, sore and cold and in the next few hours she would be having a baby. How had she been so stupid? She had hardly shown but she hadn't had her monthly's for as long as she could remember and every so often a flutter like butterflies passed across her stomach. She knew she was pregnant. She had told Davy as soon as she could and he didn't want to know. He was away on the boats. He worked for the fishermen all the time now and was never in when she called round. They were seventeen, just kids themselves. Her mother would kill her if she found out. She would be the talk of the village if it got out. And, it would get out. People here were not averse to a bit of gossip. She had only told Davy. No one else, not even Evie her best friend. People would eye her, she knew, but she wore baggy clothes and it also helped that she had always been a bit chunky. The pain in her abdomen came again and she bit her bottom lip to stop from crying out.

She had brought a bag with a towel, a nappy which she had stolen from the toilets in the creche at the church hall on Tuesday morning. They always had a few in a basket for the young mothers group. She had bought a knitted first size rompersuit at the charity shop in Anstruther, just along the coast, no questions asked a nice little cardigan and blanket too. In the bag she also had a pair of scissors, a bin liner and her dad's thermos flask filled with warm water. She had watched a programme about having babies on television and knew what she should do. She had also taken parenting class as part of her Home Economics at school.

She needed to find somewhere out of this cold wind to prepare for the birth.

She couldn't go home. She had been in pain since she woke up this morning and had spent the day walking about in worry.

She stood up slowly and walked away from the wind and up towards the shops. Mr McIvor had his garage near the top of the steep hill and she squeezed herself through the wooden slider door into the oily smelling interior. She and Davy had met in here on many occasions. This was the only place they could get any peace and it was Davy who had loosened the slider door in his lust filled urgency to get inside one night. Probably on the night which had led to the events of the present.

Maybeth felt along the wall at hand height, until she came to the old couch. She knew the layout of this place. This was the waiting area. She had worked last summer in the office here. She felt for the old blanket that ran along the top of the couch and placed it on the seat. She laid it under her at the part of the couch which had a tear and the canary coloured foam was pushing through. She couldn't tell at this time what colour anything was, as the place was devoid of any light, save for the small line which was spilling under the door. Another larger wave of pain erupted and with it was a gush of warm water from between her legs. This was the breaking. She knew this was the waters bursting and the amniotic sac breaking up. This meant that the baby should be here soon. She really hoped that it would all happen safely. She couldn't go to the hospital. There would be too many questions and she already felt too ashamed. She was wearing a track suit and trainers with a padded coat over the top. She removed her coat and and took off her wet trousers. She had a sudden urge to push but felt it may be too soon. She paced the floor . It was about eight o'clock. She knew she was safe and alone here and it would be hours before anyone would come. Mr McIvor seldom opened before ten in the morning. He was getting on in years and business was slow due to the new, bigger garages opening along the coast.

Surely it would happen soon. She could see the streetlight dimly under the door and her eyes had adjusted to shadowy objects. She saw a desk with what she presumed was tyre pressure equipment and a toolbox on top. She walked over to the desk and felt the objects one by one. A car jack, an Axle wrench and a torch. She took the torch and switched it on. It gave off a light, which was not too bright. She kept it down low so that it wouldn't spill out through the door cracks and on to the street outside. She walked back over to the couch and lay down, gathering the blanket around her body. She must have slept for a bit until another urge to push took over her by surprise and she sat up. She rolled off of the couch and crouched down on the ground. This time, she felt something give. Avril removed her pants and felt between her legs. She felt something solid, warm and soft. The head. The baby was coming. She took the towel out of her bag and laid it beneath where she crouched. She positioned the torch beam to where the baby would come out and just as she picked up the scissors and water from the bag another push came. She dropped them onto the floor and put her two hands underneath, ready to catch the baby. With a deep groan of pain, a watery slither and a small squeak the baby arrived. Avril took a moment to catch her breath and feel the wriggling, warm, bundle in her hands before she moved into action. This was the important bit. She laid the baby on the towel and checked that it was breathing. It was and was giving off little high pitched noises and grunts. She cut the cord like she had seen on television and used the clean corner of the towel and the water from the thermos flask to clean the baby. It was a little girl. She put the nappy on her and dressed her quickly in the clean clothes and cardigan, then wrapped her in the shawl. She cleaned up the mess with the towel and put it all in the bin liner. She would drop it into a bin on the High Street. She took a label from the desk and wrote on it. She then attached it to the baby's wrist using a piece of string. She felt her legs a bit wobbly but otherwise she was OK. She had expected to be sore and weak, but she wasn't and she knew she had more to do. She picked the baby up, intentionally not looking at her face. She couldn't fall in love with her. She needed to give this baby away and looking at her would just make it harder. While she had been cleaning earlier she had allowed herself a quick look. The baby was perfect. She gave a quick shudder. She had to move. She gathered her things, put the torch off and back on the desk, placed the blanket as she had found it and left the garage. The wind had calmed and she moved up and round to the Church manse at the very top of the hill. There she put the baby on the doorstep and rang the bell. She waited until she heard someone moving and then she ran as fast as she could back down towards the harbour.

Pittenweem   June 2021

CHAPTER THREE

The next morning Maybeth woke up fresh at six. She showered and made herself a cup of tea, some muesli and chopped banana. She had brought a box of food with her not knowing what provisions would be available so far from anywhere. Taking the bowl and her cup she walked over to the window and opened the curtains. She sat at the window seat and looked out on to the harbour. She could get used to this view. It was a bright and summery fresh morning. She could see small waves rippling and the boats bobbling rhythmically above and around them. This was beautiful. This was calm. This was where she had started her life. She pushed the thought away. She would have some time to think again after her meeting. She finished her cereal and rose and carried the empty bowl and cup back into the kitchen. As she rinsed them out her phone buzzed on her bed. Leaving the dishes to drip dry she headed over and picked up her phone to see who had sent the text. It was Laura **HI M.B. JST CHECKN IN. X** Maybeth smiled and replied **HEY L, ALL OK, JUST ABOUT TO HEAD OUT FOR MEETING. WILL CALL LATER. M.B x** They always called each other by their initial when texting. It saved time Laura said. Maybeth put her phone into her bag and put on her jacket. Picking up her briefcase she headed for the door. Once outside she smoothed her skirt and jacket down. It was a neatly tailored skirt suit and had been made by one of the finest families of suit makers in London at the firms expense. She had three. The firm was good to her and over the years she had been good to it. She had sold a lot of houses for millions of pounds. Her sunny personality, keen business brain and sharp eye made her the perfect saleswoman. As she walked along the harbourside she was aware of the salty sea air, the loud screeching of the terns, the squawking of the gulls and the laughter and shouts of the fishermen, back from their sea shift with their catch for the day. These men –

she couldn't see any women – had already done a days graft and it was only twenty minutes after seven. She smiled as she walked. This really was the place to be on a day like today.

Pittenweem   October 1993

CHAPTER FOUR

Elsie Ford heard the doorbell and left the small living room in the manse to answer it. She had just had her supper and she wasn't expecting any visitors as the prayer meeting had finished at ten and the last of the kirk session had left around half an hour ago. In this parish though, the door was always open for anyone in need. Elsie loved to talk to people, to help them in their hour of need. She often comforted them and prayed with them. She had a shepherd's heart her husband said. Her husband George was a fairly modern minister for the Church of Scotland. He wore the dog collar but not the flowing robes. Elsie was the ideal wife. He did the preaching and the church committees and she did the mothers groups, the quiet counselling and the women's guild. Elsie opened the door and looked out into the night. No one was there, but she could hear the faint footsteps of someone running away. She smiled and shook her head. The local youngsters playing chap door runaway or Ding Dong Skoosh as they called it here. She was about to close the door when she looked down and saw the wriggly bundle on the ground. She gasped and bent down. It was a brand newborn baby. She read the tag that was wrapped around the baby's wrist. "Please care for my baby. Her name is Maybeth" Elsie lifted the baby and carried it into the manse. 'George' she said softly as she entered the living room where her husband sat reading. 'George, we have a visitor'.

The Reverend Ford put down his bible and looked up at where his wife stood, gently rocking the baby. 'Oh, my' was all he could think to say.

Pittenweem June 2021

CHAPTER FIVE

Maybeth stood outside the property office door and put on her face mask. She took a breath and opened the door where she immediately greeted by a smiley teenager who introduced herself as Kirsten. Kirsten asked her to take a seat at the window and she left to find her boss. Just as she had got comfortable Mark Vaughan appeared. He was late 30s, tall with short brown hair and what may have been a mask hidden smile. Handsome, Maybeth thought but not too distractedly handsome. Her eyes smiled back at him and he ushered her into his office. She went through the door and he followed her in and closed the door. The office was cosy. It held a filing cabinet, a large walnut desk which Maybeth thought looked too big for the room, a leather swivel chair on Mark's side of the desk and two walnut and green leather studded straight backed chairs on this side of the desk. Mark pointed to the seats and Maybeth sat down on the closest one. It was when she was seated that she realized that Mark Vaughan hadn't said a word to her. No greeting, no please as she made her way to his office. Everything had been done by gesture. A man of few words, Maybeth thought. She cleared her throat.

'It's nice to finally put a face to the email sender, even with a mask' she said.

'Yes, sorry. I'm not the best in the mornings. I'm OK after I've had my coffee'

As he said this, he poured a coffee from his coffee machine. She had the same one in her office. Maybe the company had shares.

'Would you like one?' he offered.

'No, thank you' she replied ' I had some tea before I left the room.'

Mark brought his coffee over to the desk and sat down. He removed the mask and Maybeth now caught the full effect of the man. He had the beginnings of a beard. Not scruffy, well groomed and a nice smile with good teeth. He caught her looking and took a sip of his coffee.

'Right, I believe we have a house to sell.'

The house in question was a cottage that was built into the rock at the West side of the harbour. It had a stunning view out over the water and had a private beach area. The owner was an American golfer who had bought it just over three years ago to be closer to the nearby golf course at St Andrews. St Andrews was a world famous course and one of the best ones to play according to the pros. The golfer, unfortunately, had taken a heart attack and died on the green in America and his wife was now selling off the property. She had left the sale in the hands of

Lawson and James who she had used to sell her properties in England. Three London Bankside luxury apartments that Laura had sold on for a cool 5.5 million and a cottage in the Cotswalds.

Maybeth and Mark spent the time sorting through the details of the cottage. The dimensions, features, fixtures and fittings, closeness to amenities and the price. Kirsten would now put the details on to the advert. They had two viewings already fixed in the diary for today and another four for tomorrow. An hour later, business complete for the moment, Maybeth left the office. She took off her mask as she walked along in the fresh warmth of the day. The first viewing would be this morning just before lunch and the second was scheduled for 3 o'clock. She had plenty of time to explore this place. As she headed back to the guestroom she passed a small café. The coffee smelled delicious and after declining Mark's offer of a cup, she now felt that she should have taken him up on the offer. She put her mask back on and opened the door to the café.

Pittenweem   October 1993

CHAPTER SIX

Avril sat by the harbour in the dark listening to the water lapping noisily against the boats and the harbour walls. She was sore and she was tired. She desperately needed to sleep. She thought about walking to Evie's and confiding in her but she knew that this would be a mistake. Anyway, what was there to tell now? The baby was gone. The only reminder was the cramps, the soft flesh of her belly and the blood. She had to get home and clean up before the house woke up. If her mum and dad were up she couldn't get her bloodied clothes and the towels she would be using for the shower into the washing machine and how would she explain it all? She got up from the bench and walked with as quick a pace as she could manage in the direction of her home.

Her house was on the harbour. It was an old maritime building, It had once been used to sell ships parts to Merchants and ship traders. It was now a three storey house. Her dad worked on the boats. He made a lot of money selling his monkfish and langoustines to fancy restaurants in the city. Her family always had fish and crabs to make salads and pies. Her mum worked at the golf course. She was a great cook and a hard worker. She was always working long hours but right now, this early in the morning she was tucked up and fast asleep. Avril's watch told her it was three eleven. Dad would be up soon. His boat left at five today. She tiptoed into the bathroom and stripped off her clothes. She could smell the metallic scent of blood and the waft of body odour nearly made her keel over. She held on to the sink until she felt steadier then turned on the shower. As she soaped herself down she felt the softness of her stomach. Yesterday, when she had looked there had been a small round bump but today it resembled a half deflated balloon. Her breasts were hard and stuff was leaking from them. She knew it was milk and didn't know how to stop it. She would have to stuff her bra until it stopped, she thought. A lump came unbidden to her throat as she thought of what had happened a few hours earlier. The soft squeaky noises as she had washed her baby. The baby. She mustn't think of her as her own. Yet, she had felt the need to name her Maybeth. She hadn't named her for anyone she knew friend or relative. She just liked the way the names sounded together. She would have to tell Davy the baby had been born but now she needed to sleep. She dried herself off and went to the kitchen, quietly. She put the clothes into the washing machine on a boil wash and poured herself a glass of water. She took two paracetamol tablets from the medicine cupboard and went upstairs to bed.

Pittenweem   June 2021

CHAPTER SEVEN

Inside the café it was quiet. The radio played softly in the background of the hissing from a well used coffee machine, the sizzling of frying bacon and the clatter of dishes being prepared for the day trippers and local customers. Maybeth took a seat by the window and picked up the menu. For a small village it had a large amount of available breakfast items. She was more accustomed to the coffee and bagel to go places in London rather than the bacon, egg, potato scone and even breakfast kedgeree that was on offer here. Fish? For breakfast. Well she had had kippers once or twice. She made up her mind quickly and looked around to see whether she should go up and place her order.

'She's through the back' a gruff voice said from behind her. She turned around and saw an old man, weather beaten and ruddy around the cheeks, grinning at her. His mask was lying on the table.

'Thank you' Maybeth replied. 'I wasn't sure if she came to the table.'

'Aye, she does.' He shook his head sadly. 'This Covid palaver has her running daft. You can't move from your table, You even have to wait until the toilets have been cleaned between customers. But, I suppose you're better safe than deid!' he said with a chuckle. Maybeth nodded back. She would keep her mask on until she had been served. 'I kent you were a visitor.' the man said. ' Debbie's on herself this morning. She'll no be a minute.' Just at that a woman's voice called from the kitchen 'I'll not be a minute!'

'See! What did I tell you?' the man laughed. 'So, what brings you here?' the man asked, taking a sip from the coffee cup that looked tiny in his large, work calloused hands. Grafters hands, Maybeth thought. Probably fisherman's hands.

'I'm selling a house for the property company I work for. I'm only here for a couple of days. You have a beautiful village.' she answered.

'Aye, there's beauty, but these winds when they come can chop you in two as quick as a wink and the rain and snow in the winter stops the breath in your body in its tracks.' The man shuddered as he spoke this last sentence with real and vivid memories of a winter suffered. 'Is it London you come from?' asked the man.

'Yes, Camden' replied Maybeth.

Just then, a petite, apron clad woman with blonde hair scraped up into a bun, wearing a t-shirt and skirt with carpet slippers came towards her. 'I can only apologise, honey, I had an incident with the toaster.' This was said while the woman in front of her flipped open a notepad and poised a pencil at the ready to write.

'I'm Debbie, what can I get for you?' Maybeth smiled behind her mask. 'Can I have the kedgeree and some brown toast and a cup of tea please, Debbie.'

'Certainly.' Debbie trilled back ' would you prefer a mug?'

'No, no a cup would be fine. Does it come with a saucer?' she asked hopefully.

'And a wee spoon.' Debbie replied making a funny stirring motion with the pencil in her hand.

'That would be lovely. Thank you.' Maybeth smiled again and Debbie walked back to the kitchen.

'Good choice' stated the man nodding his head in agreement 'She does a great fish dish does our Debbie.'

'Do you come here a lot?' Maybeth enquired

'Every day, as regular as clockwork for 20 years.' The man replied proudly.

'I'm sorry. I'm being incredibly rude. I'm Maybeth.'

'Charlie' the man replied. 'Maybeth? that's a fancy name.' the man said.

"Yes. Yes it is.' Maybeth stopped herself before she said any more. She needed to be sure she was telling the right folk. This was a small village and no doubt gossip travelled fast and far. Her friend Nuala lived in a small place too and she had heard some awful stories of tangled gossip and how it had ruined lives and relationships. She would have to approach this with caution too. After all, her birth mother might still live here. She could be late 40s now. Still young. Maybe Debbie and this man knew her, maybe Debbie was her! Without a name or anything to go by she would have to tread very carefully indeed. The only thing she knew for sure that was on her adoption file was that she had been left outside on the doorstep of the manse. Maybe she should start there.

'Are you alright, lass?' the man she now knew as Charlie asked, looking slightly worried.

'Yes, sorry. I'm fine.' Maybeth answered giving herself a shake.

'You were in a wee dwam' he said. 'A what?' Maybeth asked.

'A dwam. It means a wee daydream.' said Debbie as she walked over with a steaming cup of tea in a saucer with a wee spoon as promised. She popped it down on the table in front of Maybeth set out the cutlery for the breakfast. She then disappeared and returned seconds later with a plate of hot buttered toast and a small bowl of kedgeree. Maybeth licked her lips. She hadn't realized how hungry she was as her stomach gave a small growl. 'Thank you.' she said as she picked up her cutlery

'You are so welcome, honey.' Debbie replied as she walked back to the kitchen.

'Well, I'll no disturb you.' said Charlie, getting up to leave. 'I'll away and get my paper. It was nice meeting you.' he said putting on his jacket, mask and cap.

'You too' said Maybeth.

'Bye now.' Charlie raised his hand in a slight wave.

Maybeth returned the gesture with a slice of toast in her hand. 'Bye' she said to his retreating back. She took the triangle of toast that she was holding by the corner and bit into it. It was perfect. Still warm with the melted butter hitting the back of her teeth and sliding down her throat as she chewed on the soft bread with the chewy crust. She looked out of the window and saw Charlie and the world pass her by. She really could get used to this. She took a forkful of the kedgeree. Oh my. It was the most amazing thing she had ever tasted. The fresh saltiness of the fish mingled with a creamy sauce. It was wonderful. She added some to the toast and took a bite. She closed her eyes in a moment of sheer bliss. 'Well, that's the reaction I was hoping for'.

Maybeth opened her eyes and was embarrassed to see Debbie standing there and grinning down at her with her hands on her hip. 'It's amazing.' Maybeth said. 'It's the best thing I've ever eaten.'

'Oh, surely not, you must have some pretty tasty food in London or wherever it is that accent comes from.' replied Debbie.

'You're right. It is a London Accent. Camden to be exact and we do have some great restaurants with some great food but this…' she pointed at the empty bowl. 'This is off the scale tasty.' she gushed happily, meaning every word.

'It's an old family recipe.' Debbie said 'My grandmother made the kedgeree in great batches and mass portions to feed the fishermen when they came in from the catch. She taught me how to do it and here I am living the dream.'

Maybeth caught a sigh and a kind of sadness in Debbie's voice.

'Do you enjoy it, living here?' she asked.

'I do, but sometimes I wish I had gone when the others did.' replied Debbie. Catching Maybeth's puzzled look she added 'my friends. Some went too University or to work in the cities and some went to sea.'

'Was there a reason you didn't go?' Maybeth wondered.

'Love' Debbie replied. ' I fell in love, he went to sea and I waited for him to come back and when he did, I had taken on the café and he had brought back a wife from Malaysia and a child or two.' She sighed again. 'Anyway, I'm here now and I've perfected the world's best ever eaten kedgeree.' she gave a twinkling laugh and winked at Maybeth. 'I'll bring you the bill when you're ready, unless you want anything else?'

'No, the bill will be fine.' Debbie raised her hand in a wave and walked to the till where she had left the order pad. The mood had shifted. Something in Debbie had definitely saddened and Maybeth had felt her pain. Poor Debbie. Waiting for something that no longer existed. She drained her teacup and put on her mask. Debbie brought the bill and Maybeth paid with her contactless card. She thanked Debbie and left the cafe. She made her way to the guest house to freshen up before she had to leave for the first property viewing.

Pittenweem October 1993

CHAPTER EIGHT

Avril woke up to the sound of seagulls and a horn blasting. The boats were in and the men could be heard chattering and shouting as they emptied the nets and the creels. They were across in the weigh house. This was where they went daily to see how much they had made and to sell the catch on.

The pain hit her as she sat up. An emptiness washed over her and she lay back down. Tears came in a torrent onto her pillow. She put her hand up and covered her eyes. The other hand she used to cover her mouth to try and silence the sobs and gasps which she couldn't seem to stop. What was wrong with her? She had known the baby wasn't hers. She knew she had done the right thing. So why was this happening? And why wouldn't it stop?" She moved the pillow from under her head and put it over her face. There was a knock on her bedroom door followed by her mothers voice. " Avril!. Are you there?" She didn't answer. Avril?" Avril let out a groan. Her mum opened the door and entered the room. The groan had been interpreted as an indication that Avril wanted her to come in. 'What's wrong?' Avril's mum asked.

'I don't feel well.' She answered. 'Is it the flu ?' mum asked stepping out of the room. 'No', answered Avril strongly. 'Just stomach pain, I think its my period.' She added.

'Well, there's paracetamol in the cupboard in the kitchen. I'll see you tonight.' And with that she was gone. Avril waited almost an hour before she got up and went to the bathroom. She showered again and got dressed in baggy tracksuit bottoms and a thick arran knit sweater. She made her way downstairs into the kitchen. The clock on the wall said nine forty three. Davy would be off the boat now. She had to tell him what had happened. She suddenly had a horrible thought. What if nobody had answered the doorbell last night? What if the baby was still on the doorstep, or worse. She had to know. She put on her jacket and left the house. Hurrying now, as she raced up the hill towards the manse.

Pittenweem June 2021

CHAPTER NINE

The first viewing lasted two hours. It was for a young couple from the Scottish Borders who wanted to move East and settle to begin a family. He worked nearby and she worked from home. They had taken an abundance of photographs and asked all the right and relevant questions. They had loved the house indoor space but Maybeth sensed that the woman wasn't entirely settled on the seaview. As they were nearing the end of the viewing, the woman asked if she could go and sit in the car. Maybeth and the man talked price and the man said that they would have to sell first before even looking to put an offer in. Maybeth explained that the price for this property was fixed and the owner wanted a first come, first served sale. She wasn't interested in bidding wars she had said so the house would be a very quick sale. The man looked over at his wife who he could see was scrolling through her phone through the windscreen. 'I'm sorry.' he said to Maybeth. 'She doesn't want to move anyway, especially during a pandemic.' Maybeth was so used to this even without a pandemic which had slowed the market and stopped viewings for nearly a year. They had only started back with real viewings. Everything had been put online and viewings had been done by Zoom. One partner was always setting their heart on something, the other partner torn by loyalty to family or friends. She was so glad she was single. She had had a couple of close calls into matrimony, but , it wasn't to be. She enjoyed her freedom, the not having to consider another person when she had a sudden urge to do something. Nuala had once told her that home was a feeling, not a place. She hadn't known how to answer as she had never felt at home anywhere, even though she had had amazing parents.

She thanked the man and watched him go back to his car. He climbed in and gave is wife a kiss on the forehead. Maybeth closed up the house, set the alarm and locked the doors and drove back towards the harbour.

Pittenweem   October 1993

CHAPTER TEN

The manse was empty when Avril reached it and there was no baby on the doorstep. Avril breathed a sigh of relief. Someone had picked her up. Tears came suddenly to her eyes and she swatted them away hurriedly. What were they exactly? The baby had been found. She looked for the minister's Datsun Sunny car but it wasn't there. Avril took this a sign that Mrs. Ford and the minister were on the way to give the baby to the right people. *The* baby, not *her* baby. She had given up the right to call her hers when she rang that doorbell and walked away. Maybeth would be Maybeth no longer. Someone else would name the child. Avril made her way down Kirkgate and onto Cove Wynd which led down towards the harbour. Davy lived just off the East Shore harbour at the bottom of Cove Wynd with his mum and dad, older brother, Fraser and twin sister Davina. Davina and Avril had been friends since nursery school but she had a boyfriend now and Avril had Davy. Davy's dad and Fraser would be out at sea just now but Davy was home. She reached the front door which was a deep blue colour. All the houses here had pastel or bright coloured doors and some even had pink or yellow brick. The village was popular with artists and creatives. Avril knocked on the door and was greeted by a 'Come away in, Avril the door's open.' from Davy's mum. She opened the door onto a homely kitchen area where Davy's mum stood at the stove. The house was small but very welcoming. A warm heat came from the Aga where Mrs. McCreath was making pancakes. 'Long time, no see, pet' Mrs. McCreath said 'He's through in the other room.' She handed Avril a plate with a freshly made pancake on it. The steam was still gently rising as she took it from the smiling woman. Avril thanked her and walked through to where Davy was sitting on a two-seater sofa watching T.V. He looked at her and warily eyed her up and down, until his gaze finally settled on her stomach. 'what do you want?' he said with a sigh. 'We need to talk.' Avril said firmly. 'I've told you, Avril. I can't do it.' he whispered angrily. 'It's done.' Avril said matching his tone and picking at her pancake. 'A girl, yesterday. I called her Maybeth. She's gone now.' Avril stopped speaking and looked up at Davy. Davy was staring at her with a puzzled look on his face. 'Mum!' he shouted, taking Avril by the wrist none too gently. 'I'm going out.' He marched himself and Avril out of the front door. 'You're hurting me, Davy.' Avril groaned as they let the door slam behind them. Davy let go of Avril's wrist. 'I'm sorry…it's just…I don't know what you mean.'

They started to walk. 'Let's find somewhere to sit and talk' Davy said gentler now.

They walked in silence to the small inlet at the East end of the harbour where a bench sat for thinkers and poets. They settled on the bench and looked out on to the rippling water. Loud terns competed with each other as Avril fed them the pancake she had carried in sweating hands from the house. Avril broke through the noise with her own voice. 'I had the baby, Davy. I just needed you to know.' she paused waiting for him to speak. When he didn't, she continued. 'I left her on the manse doorstep and rang the bell.' Tears started to fall swiftly now 'she must have been found because I've just been back to check and she's not there.' Silence fell again and even the terns had stopped. Avril tried to stem the tears. Was this part of the childbirth experience? Did she have the baby blues? She had an aunty Marjory who had the baby blues after her cousin Douglas was born. She had cried for ages. Her mum had dodged a few visits with her as it had got on her nerves. The silence stretched until Avril could stand it no more. 'Aren't you going to say something?"

'What is there to say? We'll just need to be more careful next time.' Davy answered sullenly.

Avril's mouth opened in shock. 'next time?' she answered loudly 'do you seriously think there is ever going to be a next time?' She stood up and faced him. 'You treated me like dirt, refused to help me through this while thing – which, by the way you were half responsible for and now have nothing to say.' She took a breath and started to back away from him. 'I don't ever want to see you again Davy McCreath.' and then she turned on her heels and ran.

Pittenweem   June   2021

CHAPTER ELEVEN

Maybeth found herself back in Debbie's café the next morning. She had another viewing pencilled in for two o'clock this afternoon and she had closed on three sales online before nine this morning. It was just after half past nine and here she was ordering a coffee and eggs benedict and looking out once again on to the harbour at the boats bobbing about almost happily she thought. The bobbing was quite relaxing. It should have been unsettling, the non - rhythm as the waves rushed and lapped from all sides, but she found it quite calming. She wondered if her birth mother had ever looked out on to this same scene. Of course she would have, there wasn't really anything else to do in this place. Maybe that was why her mother had got pregnant. Boredom. Maybeth sighed deeply. 'My! That was a sigh and a half.' A voice declared from behind her. 'Care to share?' said Debbie, who had been filling sugar containers and salt and pepper shakers at the counter. Maybeth half-smiled. 'I'm just having a moment.' she answered. 'It is beautiful here' she continued.

'Have you been here before?' Debbie asked, her eyes still on her task. She had to concentrate as it was not the first time she would have poured sugar into the salt shaker and salt into the sugar sifter. Maybeth watched her for a moment. Should she open up to this woman? She seemed kind enough, but what if she opened up and Debbie knew her family? What if Debbie *was* her family? Was she really ready to do this, open this big can of worms? Before she knew what had come over her she told Debbie everything she knew. Debbie had finished her pouring and was now sitting opposite her wide eyed and open mouthed under her mask and visor.

'Are you alright?' Maybeth asked her with concern etching her own face. Debbie gulped back emotionally and replied 'that is the most heartbreaking thing I've ever heard.' Maybeth thought it must be pretty sad after hearing Debbie's story. Debbie shook her head as though to clear the feelings that had swamped her as she listened to Maybeth. 'So do you have any idea what you want to do about it?' She asked

Maybeth.

'I didn't come with a game plan. I was asked to sell a house here and to be perfectly honest with you, I've never really thought about my past or my roots. I had such an amazing upbringing I had forgotten all about who my birthparents might be.' This was a lie, Maybeth had thought about them on and off throughout her life, especially during her teenage years. She had had feelings of abandonment and questions about who she looked like, what her parents were doing now, why they had left her on a doorstep.

To be fair he hadn't dwelt on it but they had been there. Like a cobweb in a corner waiting to be cleaned up. 'I could help you if you want. I've read all of Val McDermid's books. I like a bit of mystery.'

'Is she not a crime writer?' Maybeth asked. 'Aye, but still.' Debbie giggled 'you know what I mean.'

'I think I would like that.' Maybeth replied with a smile. 'Is there a place that has parish records or do you know if the minister and his wife are still around? That might be a starting point.'

'I'm not sure about the minister, but, the hall up at the top of the hill on the main street, which is the community hub now, should have some school or parish records from the 1990's. Is it a school roll you are looking for?'

'It would be helpful I think. Even just getting a name would be nice.' Maybeth smiled again and Debbie looked out of the window, deep in thought.

'You have such a familiar face, I just wish I knew who you belonged to.' Maybeth shrugged and let out a small laugh. 'It felt good to share that actually. Thank you Debbie.'

Debbie stood up. 'I haven't done anything yet, but leave it to D.I. Debbie.' Maybeth laughed again. 'I could murder another cup of tea please detective.' she said. 'Coming right up.' replied Debbie as she walked away still giggling and tapping the side of her nose.

Pittenweem   October 1993

CHAPTER TWELVE

Avril was angry. She was so very angry. How dare he. She had known Davy her entire life. She was crying a steady stream of tears as she ran back up and away from the harbour. Away from Davy. She had past the Mid Shore and was heading to the house on the rock at the other end of the harbour. Davy had been so heartless there. So uncaring. How had she been so stupid as to let him near her. He didn't love her and he certainly wouldn't love her baby. She had reached the end of the lido and was walking along the sand and rocks at the waters edge. The gulls were calling loudly, taunting her, laughing at her. She threw her head back and screamed until she thought her lungs would burst. She was exhausted. She sat down on the cold, wet sand, her eyes nipping with strain and salt air and looked blindly out to sea. She had to leave. She had to try and get a job out of here. She was seventeen. She could apply for a college course in the city. Her mum would allow it she was sure. With the start of a plan starting to form in her mind she stood up and headed for home. She would work it all out. She didn't need Davy McCreath, she didn't need this place. She had her whole life ahead of her and she wasn't going to waste another second. As she walked back, her head lifted, her strides became more meaningful and she felt a quiet determination start to increase in volume. She would make something of her life so that when her daughter came looking for her she would be ready to be a mum. She smiled at this and was still smiling when she reached her front door. She pushed it open and heard her mum whistling some pop tune in the kitchen. She went in to join her, whistling along as she went. 'Someone's in a happy mood.' Mum said. 'What's up?'

'Nothing's up, Mum.' Avril replied

'Are you hungry?' Mum asked offering a plate of pancakes.

'Starving.' she answered taking two off the plate and stuffing them into her mouth. The last one had gone to the terns. No-one was getting these. Mum giggled and Avril giggled too. Yes, everything would be alright.

Pittenweem   June 2021

CHAPTER THIRTEEN

The Community Hub was not what Maybeth had expected. She had thought it would be full of bustle and noise. Instead, there was a middle-aged woman in a love heart face mask sitting behind a desk. There were two women drinking coffee from polystyrene cups while two toddlers clambered on an indoor climbing frame and rolled over soft play furniture under a sign that declared that the furniture and play equipment would be sanitized after every session and only people with close family contact were allowed at a time with 3 CHILDREN MAX in huge letters. On closer inspection the two women looked alike so were probably sisters, Maybeth surmised. A man in a polo shirt, jeans and blue gloves was sitting near the fire exit armed with some cleaning materials and a box of masks. He was obviously on hand to clean between play sessions and to make sure that people followed the rules and left by the fire exit when they went.

The women barely looked up as Maybeth walked by them but the one at the desk had straightened herself up in preparation for a chat. 'This was probably the only conversation this woman would have all day' thought Maybeth. It was a good thing it wasn't busy. Busy meant no time but this woman looked as if she had all the time in the world. 'Hello, How can I help you?' the woman asked in a small, trilling, birdlike voice. 'I really hope you can.' Maybeth spoke up in a friendly tone. " I'm looking for a school rolls from about 1991 to 1993."

'Hmm.' replied the woman thoughtfully, putting her finger to where her lip would be behind the mask. '1990's, yes it should be around here.' The woman had bent down under the desk and was rifling through a drawer in a low filing cabinet. She seemed to find what they were looking for and sat back up clutching a cardboard file.

'Now, before I let you see it, I need to know why you need to see it.' the woman said.

Maybeth noticed that the woman's tone had become more officious but the twinkle in her eye still remained. The woman was nosy but she was right to be cautious and GDPR meant that she needed to know. Maybeth could be anyone. She took a breath and let the woman in on her story. When she had finished the woman was giving her much the same look as Debbie had given her.

'My, that's quite a tale. Let's see what we can find out on these papers. I can only give you names.' She held up the file and opened it up revealing a bundle of papers. 'Now, what are you hoping to find?' the woman asked gently.

'I honestly don't know.' Maybeth answered 'if I get names I can start there, but I don't really know how to go about this.'

The woman smiled gently under the mask. 'Let's have a look. We'll see if we can get you some answers. Now, you reckon the woman who was your birth mother would have been a teenager?'

'I don't know.' sighed Maybeth ' I don't know what age she was. I really am at a loose end. I just thought we could start there.'

They looked through the papers wearing rubber gloves and staying apart. The woman reading out names and Maybeth jotting them down. All the girls would have been between fifteen and eighteen. It didn't take too long. Only 63 registered from 1991 to 1993. Maybeth looked at her watch. It was 1pm. She had a viewing scheduled for 2pm. She thanked the woman and bought a cheese scone and a caramel wafer from the small café area to the woman's right. She was in charge of that too. As she walked away from the building, Maybeth thought she heard someone calling her name. She looked around but couldn't see anyone. She continued walking down towards the harbour, eating her scone as she walked. She hadn't used her car since she arrived, preferring to walk up and down the steep streets. It was revitalizing and a lot cheaper than the gym. The scone was delicious. She could taste a bit of mustard through it. She was always eating on her feet. Laura was forever getting on at her for it. It was bad for her, she knew, but she had so much to do, and she had just added a whole heap more. She finished the scone and took her phone out of her pocket and dialed Laura's number. She updated her on the house and shared some small talk before she got to the next viewing. The couple hadn't arrived when she got there so she let herself in and sat down on a kitchen stool, looking out to the choppy waters below. The doorbell rang about five minutes later and she put on her professional face behind the mask as she answered it. Two men in their early fifties stood with smiling eyes at the door. 'Hi. I'm Maybeth.' Maybeth welcomed as she ushered them inside. She showed them every inch of the house with her usual flair. The men were both working in the city but eager to move to a more sedentary lifestyle by the sea. They seemed charmed with the space and by the location. Maybeth felt a little sad because if this house was sold too quickly she would have to continue the search for her mother, online, back down in London and not at the scene. When the men had seen all that they needed to see and asked all that was needed to ask, the men said that they would be in touch and left. Maybeth stood for another few minutes in the empty house and again was drawn to look out the window. The day was beginning to darken, storm clouds were gathering. The waters were certainly looking a lot angrier now too. She locked up and walked hurriedly towards her guest room. She had to write up this viewing and then she would pour herself a large glass of wine and pore over the notes she had taken at the community Hub.

Glasgow   June 1994

CHAPTER FOURTEEN

The train was empty when Avril got on. She had taken the bus from the harbour into the nearest town with a train station. There she had boarded the train to Glasgow City. This was it. She had spent the last few months writing letters to employers in the city and she had now managed to secure an apprenticeship. She was going to work in a jeweler's shop.

She would learn on the floor with the jeweler's and attend college one day a week for two years. Her mum and dad had been delighted and had phoned her Aunty Morag, who lived in the city and had offered her somewhere to stay if she ever decided to leave home. Aunty Morag was her mum's sister. She was an artist and had a studio in the trendy West End. Avril loved her pictures. They were colourful and always had a wee stag in the corner beside her signature. It wasn't only Aunty Morag's art that was trendy. She was trendy too and had loads of interesting friends. She had always fascinated Avril and regaled her with many tales of her exciting life. Aunty Morag was meeting her off the train. Avril sat back and looked out of the window at the countryside battering past at speed. She thought about the last few months and wondered if the baby was in the city too. She was still angry at Davy. He had tried to come and see her, he even bought her a Christmas present, but she refused to see him. This was for the best. A new start in a new place. She laid her head on the headrest and let her mind empty. She must have dozed off only waking when she heard the sharp blast of a whistle and the train started to slow. She looked out of the window on to the platform. There was Aunty Morag jumping up and down with glee and waving her arms. Avril laughed and waved back. She took her two bags of luggage from the luggage rack and jumped down from the train. She walked towards the exit where

Aunty Morag was waiting with her arms out. When Avril got to her, she put the bags down and threw herself into her arms, where she promptly burst into tears.

Pittenweem   June 2021

CHAPTER FIFTEEN

Judy Kay, Avril McKay, Catriona Blyth, Evelyn Dunne, Davina McCreath. The list went on and on. Why had Maybeth thought this would lead anywhere? She finished her wine and took the empty glass over to the sink where she washed it and left it on the draining board. It was just going on for six in the evening and the cheese scone she had eaten at lunchtime had long since been absorbed. She grabbed her jacket. She knew that Debbie did some fine evening meals too.

When she got to the café, Debbie pointed to a table with a reserved sign on it. 'I thought you'd be in.' she shouted over the noise of cutlery, coffee machine and chat. 'Take a seat and I'll get you once I've seen to tables five and seven.'

Maybeth smiled under her mask. She was becoming a regular. The smile died a little when she remembered that she would be going home soon. She had brought the list with her just in case any of the names rang familiar with Debbie.

Later, when the café had emptied and only Maybeth and Debbie remained, they sat and studied the list intensely. 'I think I know all the names, but they are a fair bit younger than me. They have all either left long ago or died.' Debbie murmured. 'Davina McCreath was Davy McCreath's twin sister. She died last year. Davy is still here. He works on the boats. In fact, he would have known all the girls at that time, that's if the woman you are looking for was even that age.'

'I know.' Maybeth replied despondently. 'She could have been an older woman, or married and it could have been an affair, or something worse.' Maybeth looked at Debbie who nodded sadly. They were both thinking that perhaps her beginning had been more tragic and she had been the result of a crime. Maybeth had thought that over the years too, always pushing it out before it could really upset her. She sighed loudly.

'This is hopeless isn't it. It's like looking for a needle in a haystack.'

'I'm not giving up and neither should you.' Debbie said defiantly.

'It's just that I'm leaving for home in a few days. The house is nearly sold. I can't be here to look into anything else. As much as I would have liked to.' Maybeth put her head into her hands. 'I think I just need to forget about it until I have more time.'

'And what if your mother is here? What if she doesn't have the time and what if she has all the answers to everything you need to know about where you came from?' persisted Debbie. 'Come on, Maybeth. This is exciting. Have you no holidays to take?'

Maybeth smiled and shook her head. 'I never take holidays.'

'So, you should take one now!' Debbie laughed encouragingly. 'Go on.'

'OK' Maybeth sighed but with a sudden giggle that surprised her. 'I'll see what I can do.'

'Right.' said Debbie 'That's settled. How about a wee glass of apple juice to start the holiday. Unfortunately, we are not allowed to serve alcohol just now.'

'Ruddy Covid' Maybeth laughed. 'My holiday hasn't started yet, I still have a house to sell, but a wee glass of apple juice sounds good.'

'See.' said Debbie 'You're starting to sound like a local already.'

Glasgow   April 1995

CHAPTER SIXTEEN

It had been a year since Avril had started her apprenticeship and she was really enjoying it. The hours were long and that was a good thing as she had less time to think about the past. She had made some friends here. Louise and Angie worked alongside her and Jemma worked in the music shop next door. They always had a quiet drink on a Friday evening after they had finished work. Jemma had a boyfriend called Billy who sometimes joined them with his pal, Chris. Louise and Angie were both married. Louise had two teenage daughters, but Avril had no wish to get involved with anyone. She had learned her lesson. Louise and Angie were always asking her about her upbringing. What was it like growing up in a small place? Did they have electricity there? Being city girls, they thought that small harbour villages were alien landscapes. Avril teased them by telling them that people had extra fingers for gutting the fish. When they asked where hers was, she told them she had managed to escape it before the growth age of twenty. She would be twenty next year. Right now, she was sitting on her bed reading, in her room in the centre of the city looking down on the busy street below. Aunty Morag's flat was just off one of the busiest shopping streets and it was really handy for everything. Shops, bus stops, take aways and even the doctors surgery was a stones-throw away. Avril loved the city. She loved the hustle and bustle, the banter of the vendors and buskers, the noise of the traffic and the whole symphony of city sound. She phoned her mum once a week. Mum had wanted her to go to college and keep up her education and Avril was currently looking through prospectuses to see if she could take a night class. There were a few that caught her eye, but she wasn't sure yet which one to apply for. Dental nursing,

Retail management or Hospitality? She shut the book over, got up and went to stand by the window. It looked like it was a nice day. It was the Easter holiday's and the town was bustling with locals and tourists. She grabbed her coat and decided to go to the Art Gallery and Museum on the other side of the city. She loved it there. There was always so much to see and it was free too. Aunty Morag was at her studio and wouldn't be back for hours. Avril locked the door and danced down the stone stairs, out of the close and out into the street. The sun was quite warm but there was still a spring chill. She was glad she had put her coat on. She had a wooly beret in her pocket, so she took it out, gave it a quick shake and put it on. She caught the number seventy-seven bus that took her to just outside the museum and sat back in her seat looking out at the bustling pavements. Retail Management she thought suddenly. She would discuss it with Aunty Morag tonight. She watched the landscape change as she neared the museum. This part of the city had a beautiful park, and the trees and greenness of the area always made her smile. The bus stopped and Avril got off and walked the sixty yards or so to the grand set of steps that led up to the museum building, It truly was a magnificent building. It was built in 1901 and made from a red sandstone. Avril loved to come here at any time of day, but at sunset, the building looked particularly radiant and the red sandstone was illuminated in all its glory. She took in a contented breath as she walked up the steps. She would grab a coffee and a custard cream before she looked about. This was becoming quite a ritual. ' This is becoming quite a ritual.' a voice said from behind her as she sat down in the café area with her tray. Avril looked up. It was Chris, Jemma's boyfriends pal. 'Oh, hiya.' she said with a smile. 'What are you doing here?' she asked. He grinned at her and paused slightly before answering her. 'I work here. I've seen you loads of times, but I'm usually up there.' He pointed to where a huge pipe organ stood grandly fixed into the wall. It towered over the ground floor atrium. Chris didn't wear a uniform but was instead dressed in a smart suit. He was wearing a badge that stated "Organist".

Avril had heard the organ played a number of times and it was wonderful. It was one of the reasons she loved this place so much. The timbre and hum pouring out fugues, preludes, hymns and sonatas were beautiful and she always felt calm and entranced by what she heard.

'Is it you that plays all these wonderful pieces?' she asked incredulously. Chris laughed. 'You look shocked . Yes, guilty as charged.' Avril stared at him with her mouth wide open. Chris started to look a little worried. "Are you OK?"

Avril shut her mouth. 'Sorry.' she whispered 'I love that music.' She smiled at him in awe. 'You are amazing.' She gushed ' I didn't know you were a musician. You never said.'

'You've never asked.' Chris said sadly. Avril felt the mood shift. 'Do you want to join me? I'm just having this before I look around.' she said pointing at her slowly cooling coffee.

'You must know this place inside and out by now.' Chris said brightening. " I probably do, but it'll never get old.' They both laughed as she realized what she had said.

'Old, in a museum.' Chris chuckled. 'You're funny, but…' The smile left his face 'I would have loved to join you but unfortunately I have to go and play a nocturne.'

'Oh, that's great. I mean… It's not great as in not joining me, but…' Chris put his hand up as Avril's face turned pink. What was wrong with her?

Chris spoke 'Maybe we could meet later?' Avril paused then nodded. She would like that. Chris seemed interesting and she wanted to know more about his job. It fascinated her. 'Are you free tonight?' he finished.

'Yes, I can meet up with you tonight.' She replied.

'Great. There's a nice wee fish café on Albion Street.' Chris suggested.

'Yes, I know it. It's just a fifteen minute walk from where I stay.' Avril said.

'Meet you there at six? ' Chris ventured.

'Six is good.' Avril smiled. 'See you there.' And with a smile and a wave he was gone.

Avril bit her lip and smiled. What had she done? She was going on a date. With a man. Chris was probably a year older but not much more than that. She finished her custard cream and was halfway through the coffee when the first note of the organ started. She looked up and there was Chris with his back to her. She could see his face in the little mirror, she thought she caught him wink at her. He was up there playing to his audience, enrapturing the crowd with the magical sounds. She felt a warmth seep through her and not just from the coffee. She was looking forward to this evening very much.

Pittenweem   June 2021

CHAPTER SEVENTEEN

Laura had been happy for Maybeth to take a holiday. 'This sounds so exciting.' she had told her when she called to ask for the time. 'Sort of like a cross between Miss Marple and Davina McCall.' Maybeth had laughed. The thought had crossed her mind too. She was familiar with the popular TV programme *"Long Lost Families"* which scoured records until they found the lost family members of people. Sometimes they even had to go abroad to unite them. Maybeth smiled to herself as she thought what could happen in her situation. As suddenly as the smile appeared it started to die as she realized the enormity of the task. Her mother, if she had been young, could be abroad herself. Perhaps she had a new family and a new life in Australia, New Zealand, the U.S. What then? Could she go back to pushing her to the back of her mind again? She didn't think that was possible. She got up from the chair she had sat on to make the call and made the decision to have a day further along the coast. Exploring. This was now a holiday. Official. She unplugged her laptop and zipped it back into its case. It deserved a holiday too. Laura had said she would deal with enquiries for the house. Maybeth was to take two weeks break and they would resume the viewings from there. Maybeth liked that idea. It would mean longer. The Old Chandlery rental had been booked for 6 weeks so that gave her a bit of time after her holiday too. Maybeth chose a lemon tunic top and a pair of light wash jeans for the day. She slipped on her favourite flat footwear, a well worn but still immaculate pair of doc marten boots in a floral pattern. She threw on a denim jacket to complete her look, grabbed her bag and headed outside. Maybeth walked to her car and unlocked the door. It was a lovely crisp, clean day. She could feel the air starting to warm. The water moved silently, but the now familiar noise of the sea birds was still resounding in the blue skies. As she sat in the driver's seat, she became aware of a man standing looking in at her from a distance, curiously. He seemed oddly familiar. As she drove passed him, she recognized the face and as she looked at herself in the car mirror she knew immediately why that was.

Glasgow   April 1995

CHAPTER EIGHTEEN

The chips were so hot that Avril had to shuttle them round her mouth. The were delicious, with just the right amount of salt and vinegar. Avril had grown up with fish and chips as a staple of the harbourside and she had never grown tired of the taste. 'These are so good.' She exclaimed as she swallowed the mouthful. 'It's a hidden gem this place.' said Chris 'people walk by or only come in for things to take away. They have no idea that there are these tables through the back.' He swept a hand around the small, other than themselves, empty area where 4 little tables with matching chairs in an art deco design were tastefully spaced. 'I found it when I was at the Academy of Music.' continued Chris. 'It opened late so was ideal for after concerts and study.'

"The Academy of Music. That sounds so grand and exciting." Avril mused.

"It is exciting and the concert halls are grand but its extremely hard work. As I'm sure your job is too.'

Avril smiled. 'I enjoy the selling and the customer service, but training can be hard. Learning about weight, how to measure, where the gems in the jewelry originate from, what to look for in a quality stone, studying watch magnetisms, learning the names of watchmakers." She looked at Chris who was smiling widely at her. 'I'm going on a bit, aren't I?'

'No, you are fascinating.' He said breathily not taking his eyes from her. 'Have you finished?' he asked?

'No.' she answered. 'I could go on and on about my job for days.'

'I meant your tea.' Chris said.

'Oh…yes!' Avril blushed feeling foolish.

Chris stood and took his jacket from the back of his chair. Avril did the same. 'Where to now?' Chris asked.

'Ehm, did you want to do something else?' Avril asked.

She had presumed the meal was all this date would consist of.

'Well the night is still young. Do you want to go for a drink or take a walk by the river for a bit? I'm enjoying your company Avril, and to tell you the truth, that doesn't happen very often.' He said this all in a rush and Avril stared at him. She was enjoying herself too and really didn't want to go home yet either. 'The river walk sounds good.' she said ' I don't really like drinking on a night when I've got work in the morning.'

'Then, shall we?' Chris presented his arm to her, and she took it laughing as they left the table. Chris paid the bill after a stern "don't even think about going for your purse" which had made Avril laugh even more. The evening continued in laughter. Avril felt her cheeks and jaw starting to hurt, but she didn't want the night to end. Soon enough it did with Chris escorting her back to her door. 'I've had a lovely time. Can we do this again?' he asked as they stood in the light of the overhead close light. Avril smiled shyly. She had never done this bit before. With Davy they had been pals, so saying goodbye had always been easy as they knew they would do the same tomorrow.

Davy. Why had he popped into her head right now. She felt her smile slip and shook her head unconsciously. Chris noticed and took a step back. 'or if you'd rather not...' he stammered looking hurt. 'No, no. I would like it. I really had a great time Chris. Thank you. I'm just a bit tired.' She knew he had seen the change and now all she wanted to do was go inside and give herself a good talking to.

'Goodnight' he said, looking at her with a puzzled smile. 'Goodnight.' she said back but didn't move. 'What?' he asked 'Are you waiting for something?' His voice cracked with nervous emotion.

'Yes.' she answered. 'Your phone number. Or do I have to get it from Jemma?'

Chris let out a chuckle as he looked at her. She had put her hand on her hip and was standing there like a petulant teenager. They were still teenagers. She was nineeen and he was nineteen and a half, but before she had struck that pose, he had been sure she was older than him. He loved that she wasn't from here. She had a life away from the city. Her accent was softer too and he had been admiring her from afar when they all gone out as a group. She seemed more mature than Louise, Angie and Jemma. There was a faraway look sometimes when she didn't know you were watching her. He had seen something happen tonight as they had finished this date.

'Hello.' he heard Avril saying.

'Oh, sorry I was miles away.' he quickly snapped out of his reverie. 'Yes, phone number. OK. Do you have any paper?' he said quickly.

Avril rummaged about in her bag and found a till receipt and a kohl eyeliner pencil. 'Best I can do" she said handing them to him.

'Although,' he retorted 'we are standing outside your flat.' Avril stood still. Should she invite him in? What was the expectation? Would he expect more. She knew boys went in for one-night stands. Chris felt the shift again and quickly wrote his number on the paper. 'Here you go.' He said ' I'll hopefully hear from you soon?' 'Definitely' she said taking the paper from him and looking down at the neat writing. 'and thanks again Chris, I

really had a great time.' She opened the door and bounded upstairs and into the flat. She ran to the bathroom and locked the door. What had happened? She went to the sink and turned on the cold tap. She dropped the phone number on the floor and bent down over the sink splashing the cold water over her face. She looked up and caught her reflection in the mirror. She stared at herself.
Davy? Where had he come from tonight? The baby? Always when she thought of Davy was baby was never far away. She picked up her things and walked towards her bedroom, listening out for Aunty Morag, but all was quiet. She must still be at the studio. She looked at the clock on the wall as she passed through the hallway on her way to her room. 9.18pm.

As she reached the room, she pulled off her jacket, threw her bag and Chris's number on the sheepskin rug, dived onto the bed and immediately dissolved into tears.

Pittenweem   June 2021

CHAPTER NINETEEN

Davy McCreath was still staring long after the little red car had gone. He had been waiting for the harbour hall to open to collect more crab creels when he had looked up and locked eyes with the lass in the sports car. He knew instantly who she was. She had never been far from his thoughts. He had always wondered what had happened to her. Had Avril reconnected with her? Had she grown up knowing who he was? Why was she here? There was no mistaking that face and the surety he felt immediately had hit him like a thunderbolt. Avril had left not long after she had given the baby up. He had been heartbroken when she left but he was only a boy and at that time he had not given enough thought to the reality and gravity of what had happened. He had missed Avril every day, but she had left him. He had spent all those years out on the boats. He had never met anyone, never had any more children. He felt sad that the only child he had fathered he had never set eyes on. 'Are you alright, Davy?' a voice called from across the road. It was Debbie from the café. 'You look like you've just seen a ghost.' She chuckled.

'I think I may well have done.' Davy replied.

'Have you got time for a coffee?' Debbie ventured. Davy smiled. He was ready to get this off his chest. He had spent twenty odd years running from it all. There wasn't much Debbie didn't hear in that café. Perhaps she knew where the girl had come from, where she stayed, who she was. He pushed himself away from the wall he was leaning on and crossed the road. 'You better make it a large mug' he said as he put on his mask and walked over to join her.

Edinburgh   June 1998

CHAPTER TWENTY

Chris paced up and down the waiting room nervously. He had just been called to get here as quickly as possible. A door opened and a young nurse appeared. 'Mr. Hargrave ?' she asked. 'That's me.' Chris said rushing over to her. 'You have my wife, Avril.' he hurried on nervously. The nurse smiled 'Yes, I'll just take you through.' she ushered Chris through the double doors. 'She is in theatre, so we'll just get you gowned up and you can go and assist.'

'Assist?' Chris gulped. The nurse giggled. 'I mean assist her emotionally. Just reassure your Mrs. Hargrave that she's doing great, and you are there for her until the little one makes an appearance.' 'Oh, right yes, that's fine. I think I can do that.'

The nurse left Chris with an auxiliary and he was gowned up and taken through to the theatre. Avril lay on the operating table with a heart monitor beeping, surgical tools on a sterile table beside her and hospital lights blazing. The whiteness encircling her. A midwife in scrubs and the nurse who had collected him stood chatting to Avril as Chris walked in. 'It's the man of the moment.' The midwife said. 'Just in time by the looks of things too.' Avril let out a groan and Chris rushed to her side. 'It's Ok. I'm here.' He said quietly. 'Thanks love.' Avril responded. 'and I'm staying with you' he added looking deeply into her eyes. After their first date, Avril had taken things slowly with Chris. He had got a great job at St Giles Cathedral in Edinburgh as the organist and was also teaching music privately and Avril had moved through to be with him, finding a job in a large jewelers company and going back to college to get more highers. On her 20th birthday, Chris had proposed. They had a small wedding at St Giles and a meal with Avril's mum, dad, gran and Aunty Morag and Chris's mum, dad and two brothers who Avril loved at first sight. They were twins and had a wicked sense of humour. They both lived in Edinburgh too. Andrew was married to Heidi and Luke was still finding himself and having fun in the process, according to him.

Avril had also told Chris about her baby. When she had moved in with him, the need to impart the secret had become too irrepressible. It had come tumbling out one evening as they were watching a documentary about squid. No relation to anything but Avril could not shift the need to tell and so it had come out. It had not come alone. With it had arrived tears, pain and a lot of hugs and reassurances from Chris encouraging her to do whatever she needed to find her baby again, if that was what she wanted.

Another wave of pain swept through Avril's body bringing her to a place she had been to before. This was near the point. She remembered. The baby would be here soon. Chris held her hand. Right, here we go." said the midwife, positioning herself between Avril's legs. The other nurse stood back with the monitor. 'OK.' the midwife encouraged. 'I'm going to ask you to push hard and then stop and take a breath and then push again. Can you manage that?' 'Yee..sss,' said Avril through gritted teeth. Then she did exactly as she had been told to do and as the second push came, everything went black.

Pittenweem   June 2021

CHAPTER TWENTY-ONE

Maybeth parked her car in a car park along the coast in a dream. She had had to force herself to drive away when she saw that face. That face so like her own. She had to be related to that man. She had seen the shape of his eyes. They were her eyes too. His nose, her nose. Slim and long. She had always liked her nose. She had wondered where she had got it from. Maybe he was her uncle on her mothers side. Maybe on her fathers side. He looked about fiftyish, maybe late forties. It was hard to tell from the short time she had studied his face. Also, he looked boat faced and weather beaten. He could have been younger, or older. Oh, she was so confused. She would look for him again tomorrow. But, what if he was a visitor? What if, like her he was just passing through? 'Excuse me?' a voice said loudly from over Maybeth's shoulder. Maybeth looked round, half expecting to see a rugged sailor, but in his place was a young couple with a buggy containing a fractious toddler. Maybeth realized that she was in the way. She had walked from her car to the ticket machine and just stood in front of it, unseeing. 'Sorry.' She muttered letting them pass. She paid for her parking and walked towards the rock shops selling sticky pink seaside rock, candy floss, buckets and spades in hard colourful plastic wrapped in some sort of soft netting. She remembered having this when her mum and dad had taken her to Eastbourne for her holidays. She had loved it there, playing at Treasure Island, visiting the theatre, Beachy Head, (Although she had sat in the car there. She hated heights.) and the bandstand. She had once met a famous actor on the bandstand. Someone from her mothers era. She had asked him for his autograph for her mum and he sighed and said "aah, it's always for the mother." They had laughed before he left to get ready for his performance at the theatre. Her mum. What would she think of Maybeth looking for her biological family? They had loved her so much that they had kept a name link for her but they also loved her so much that they never holidayed in Scotland just in case anyone recognized her name. She loved them too. They were her mum and dad, no matter what happened. Thinking about them brought a lump to her throat and she coughed it away as she walked. She came to a little tea hut and bought herself a chai latte. She found a bench that looked out to sea and sat down to rest. The image of the man she had seen would not leave her and, as she finished her tea, she stood up, put the empty cup in a nearby bin and with purpose, strode back to her car. She needed to know where he fitted into her past.

Edinburgh   May 2003

CHAPTER TWENTY-TWO

Chris pushed Nathaniel on the swing. Nathaniel loved the swings. There were three in a row in this park and he always chose the one in the middle with the faded pink seat, rusty bolts and the small crack running around the right side. It was Nathaniel's 5th birthday tomorrow and Avril had sent Chris and the boy out while she tidied the house. This would be his last party before he started primary school so they had invited five friends from nursery, Avril's mum and dad, Andrew's boys and Aunty Morag. Avril needed a rest. She had a small hole in her heart which had been discovered when she was in the operating room after she passed out delivering Nathaniel. She was now six months pregnant with baby number 2 or 3 if you counted her daughter, and she always counted her daughter. She would be ten years old now. Avril allowed herself time to sit and think about her. What and who would she be like? She hoped every day that she had a good life. Chris was so encouraging but they had spoken to social workers who said that only Maybeth, or whatever, she was called now, could look for her but without a birth certificate to go on she would find it virtually impossible. Her baby had been a foundling. She had been found on a doorstep and quickly handed over to the authorities with no background. Only the note, written in a young person's handwriting. Avril sighed. The baby inside her gave a sharp kick and Avril smiled. Her cue, it seemed, to get back to tidying the house and binning the broken toys before the boys came back. She managed to fill two bin bags full of cracked plastic cars and polystyrene glider parts and get them out into the outside bin before she heard her giggling son and happy husband open the front door. 'Mummy!' Nathaniel shouted, running into the living room where Avril had only just sat down to rest. She grinned and held her hands out, waiting for the inevitable spring forward that always come before the tight cuddle. Nathaniel smelled of fresh grass cuttings and earthy park smells. Clean yet needing bathed. Her world. She closed her eyes and hugged him back. 'Mmm. My lovely boy.' She whispered into his hair. 'My dear, sweet, beautiful boy.' Chris came and stood beside the sofa and bent down to kiss his wife. 'Come on little man. Let's go and get something too eat.'

Nathaniel let go immediately. Food and bath time top trumped hugs every time for this one.

'There's pasta in the pot.' Avril said, smiling at the hungry child who was currently beating a hasty retreat to the kitchen with his father in tow. Her boy would be five tomorrow. She couldn't quite believe where the time was going.

Pittenweem   June 2021

CHAPTER TWENTY-THREE

'So, all those years ago you had a daughter and you've never cracked a light?' Debbie stood behind the counter as Davy sat in the booth opposite, hands wrapped around his mug of coffee, clutching it as if it was saving his life. He nodded slowly, then shook his head. ' I wish I had taken it more seriously.' He put his head in his hands. ' I should have been there for Avril.' Tears started to cloud his vision and he blinked sending one zooming down his face and on to the tabletop. He took a wipe from the tub on his table and wiped it away.

'You were only kids.' Debbie said kindly ' I do know who the girl that you saw is,

I think…and I know that she is looking for her mother.'

Davy jerked and sat up. He looked terrified. He started to feel a bit sick, and he knew he was trembling. This was going to be a huge change if it was indeed his daughter. He hadn't seen Avril since the day she had told him about the baby. He had gone out on the boat every chance he had got and a few months later someone had told him that Avril had got a job in the City. He had pretty much settled into harbour life after that, but every October he thought about the baby and Avril.

'Do you know the girl's name?' Davy asked cautiously.

'Maybeth.' Debbie answered, watching Davy's face carefully for any clues. Davy shut his eyes and nodded. 'She's mine.' He whispered softly as he began to cry.

Edinburgh   September 2010

CHAPTER TWENTY-FOUR

How dare he do this to her. Avril was furious. She had just been to see her lawyer and Chris had not made things easy for her. He was demanding more than his fair share. He was the one who had cheated. He was the one who had walked out on his family and still he was the one making all the rules. She had been hurt beyond hurt when she had discovered his betrayal. Sophie had been three and in the car when he had given "daddy's friend Melanie" a lift once too often. He had picked her up before dropping Sophie off at nursery and Sophie had told Avril that she didn't like Melanie tickling daddy's ears. When Avril had confronted Chris, he hadn't even denied it. He told Avril he wasn't happy with her and he felt trapped. He said twenty-six-year-old Melanie made him happy. Nathaniel was now twelve and Sophie, seven. She had tried to make the split easy for the children. He would let them go to Chris when he wanted to see them. She never bad mouthed him when he didn't turn up when he said he would be there, forcing the children into meltdown and wondering what they had done wrong and why daddy wasn't coming. Nathaniel's meltdowns were epic, but Sophie seemed to deal better with the break up. Perhaps because she was younger. Avril had always tried to do the right thing by them. But this, this took the fight to a whole new next level. He wanted the house. Their house. Her children's house. HIS children's house. Her lawyer had said no, she had every right to the house and could buy him out. She had the money and knew she would be staying put, but the thought of the caring man she had married turning into this almost unrecognizable being was heart crushing. She had known pain and her children deserved this fight. She picked up her mobile and started to punch in a text to Chris. **YOU SELFISH PRI** then she deleted it. She wouldn't let him see how much he had hurt her. They had been apart for nearly four years and only now had he started to change the goalposts.

'Melanie's getting fat.' Sophie had giggled after the last visit.

'I think she's pregnant.' added Nathaniel

'Does that mean we're having a sister?' trilled Sophie excitedly. ' I always wanted a sister.' Avril took a sharp intake of breath and then composed herself. It was time, she thought.

'You have a sister" she said ' come and sit down beside me and I'll tell you a story.'

Pittenweem   June 2021

CHAPTER TWENTY – FIVE

Maybeth put the key in the lock just as her phone beeped. She unmasked as she entered the room and put her bag and key on the small table beside the bed. She loved the size of this place. The living room and bedroom were one area, which made it easier to sit in either space. As she looked round she took in the rock wall which ran the length of the room opposite the front door. The bare rock made her think of the builders who had put this house together and that made her think again of the man she had seen. Not that she had been thinking of anything else since she saw him. She went to the kitchen and poured herself a glass of wine. She would nip into Debbie's in a bit but wanted to check her phone first. She went back to the living space and sat down.

She opened her phone and checked her messages. Laura was there with another offer for the Cliff House. The two men had put an offer in. She grabbed her laptop and opened up the paperwork. She then made a call to the seller and the offer was accepted immediately. With a further call to the buyers to tell them the good news the deal was done. All in the space of a few mouthfuls of wine. Three happy customers about to start a new life and one puzzled and frustrated vendor, who wasn't even thinking about the sale. That man had really put the cat among the pigeons. She hadn't set about looking for the paternal side of the family, she had forgotten there had to be a paternal side and focused all her thoughts on her mother, but the man looked so like her he had to be a relative on one side or the other. She needed to get out and speak to Debbie. Debbie would know the man. She knew everyone who lived locally. She finished her wine and rinsed the glass, used the bathroom and picked up her bag. In the time she was in she had forgotten to take off her jacket . She put her mask in her pocket and left the guest rooms. It was lovely outside. The evening was just approaching, but the warmth of the day still hung in the air. The birds were quieter now but still singing and cawing to prove they were still there. Maybeth looked over to the market, to the wall where the man had been standing. Where was he now? Where had he gone? Would he be back tomorrow? She needed to know. As she put her mask on and entered the café, she heard Debbie's voice raise, shrill with excitement. ' I told you she would turn up' she shouted. Maybeth stepped forward and Debbie stood in her path. 'Maybeth' she questioned 'do you drive a wee red sportscar?'

'Yes,' she replied 'why?'

' I told you it was her I mean there can't be two Maybeth's' Debbie was giggling now.

What was wrong with her ? Debbie seemed almost manic to Maybeth. Maybeth looked at her and realized she was talking to someone else over to her left. Maybeth followed with her eyes. It was the man. Maybeth couldn't move. Her legs felt heavy, her heart started to thump and she felt as if she would fall.

'Here' Debbie said ushering her to the table next to the man. Due to the rules on social distancing she couldn't seat her at the same table as she would have liked to.

' I think you two need to talk' Debbie said 'I'll bring you over some steak pie and veg, what do you say?'

Maybeth nodded. She didn't trust herself to speak. She couldn't take her eyes off the man, and he hadn't taken his eyes from her either. He had his mask off to eat so she was able to see his face in full. It was so like hers. The colour of eyes were blue like hers, the nose shape was like hers. The differences were in the eye shape, the cheeks, the mouth and the chin. He was smiling nervously and his eyes were watery. He looked like he would burst into tears any minute.

'Are you OK?' Maybeth asked.

'Aye, I'm fine thanks,' He continued to look at her and then asked. 'You're her, aren't you? The lassie that's trying to find her mother?' Maybeth nodded. Her eyes starting to water too. Her stomach was churning. She knew that he knew her and her life was about to change with the next question.

'Do you know her?'

The man paused. Then nodded. ' I used to.'

'Are you related to me?' she said

He nodded again. ' I am.' There was another pause, 'and I'm so happy to finally get to meet you.'

Debbie brought over the warm plate filled with steak pie, minted potatoes and garden peas and set them down in front of Maybeth.

'Isn't this lovely, father and daughter reunited.' she beamed under her mask.

Maybeth removed her mask a look of shock passing over her face.

'We hadn't got to that part yet Debbie' the man said nervously.

Debbie's mouth opened under her mask, but it was plain by the widening of her eyes how embarrassed she was.

' Oh no, I'm so sorry' she gushed, hurrying away ' I'll go and get you a drink.'

'You should have a stiff one yourself' Maybeth shouted after her.

Of course he was her father. Who else could he be?

'So" Maybeth continued, her focus back on the man, ' does this father of mine have a name?'

'Davy' he answered ' Davy McCreath.'

'Davy McCreath' she repeated ' Well Davy , where do we start?'

'You eat and I'll tell you everything I know.' He motioned with his head towards her plate. The knot had left her stomach and she took off her mask and picked up her knife and fork.

Edinburgh   May 2015

CHAPTER TWENTY – SIX

'Mum, I need to talk to you.' Nate stood in the doorway. Something wasn't right.

Avril could see it in his face. She knew instinctively when he was hurt, angry, happy or nervous and right now the eyes that couldn't meet hers were worrying a hole into the carpet.

'What's up?' Avril tried to remain upbeat, reassuring her son that whatever was wrong they could face together. Nate still didn't speak and continued to look downwards, his feet making restless tapping noises as he shuffled nervously in the doorway. His tall, lanky body narrowly missing the top beam of the door.

'Nathaniel?' Avril encouraged. He was Nate now but when he was being scolded or talked to seriously she always called him by his full name.

Nate sighed and walked into the living room. He joined Avril on the couch facing forward to avoid looking at her. He sat forward and put his hand over his face before speaking.

'Jess thinks she's pregnant.'

Avril felt her body jolt and her mind immediately went to where it always went. They sat in silence for a moment and Avril used that silence to study her son. Nate sat back and looked at the wall in front of him.

'So, what's the plan?' Avril asked quietly.

'Well obviously I'll be there for her' Nate answered just as quietly back. 'I'm not Maybeth's dad, Mum.' He continued.

Avril's eyes glistened. Things were different now and Jess and Nate were living in a much better time.

'You're both so young.' Avril smiled.

'Seventeen now, eighteen when its born.' Said Nate. Nate and Jess had become inseparable when they met in the first year of secondary school and had been dating since they were fifteen. Jess was a sensible girl. She wanted to be a pharmacist and had the brain to breeze through University. Nate was a natural photographer and was aiming to study and become a wedding and portrait photographer with his own studio.

      Nate Hargrave – Wedding & Portrait Photography

' You said Jess thinks she's pregnant. Has she done the test yet?' Avril asked.

'She's doing it when she finishes work' Nate replied ' she's coming straight over here.'

Avril nodded. Nate had told Jess all about the sister his mum had had to give away and Jess's mum would not be as understanding as Nate knew his mother would be.

'Well you know that I'm here and I'll do whatever I can to help.'

Avril could feel her mind running ahead of her. She would be a granny at thirty nine. Oh my days! Her mother had just been over forty when she had unknowingly become a grandmother. A baby would always be welcome Jess and

Nate were so young and it was like history repeating itself. Only, this time the father was present. Davy had fled and Nate was staying and would be very much a hands-on dad. If only it had been easier . Avril shook the thoughts away and stood up.

'Cup of tea?' she asked.

'Please' Nate answered taking out his phone to check his texts. Relieved that this conversation was over.

An hour later the doorbell rang. Nate bounced off the couch to answer it. Avril felt her heart start to hammer. Jess entered the room followed by Sophie and Nate. Sophie had been walking up the path as Jess drove up in her car. Jess's parents were well off and had presented her with a car for her seventeenth birthday. She had passed her tests a month ago and was a great driver already. Careful and conscientious. She sometimes picked Nate and Sophie up and took them all to school. Jess had a part time job in the chemists and went and hour after school every day and all day on a Saturday. Sophie had had a piano lesson after school so had been later than Nate at getting home.

'Hi Mum' Sophie shouted as she dropped her bag and kicked her shoes off before making for the stairs. ' I'm just going up to get changed.' She sing-songed as she noisily thumped overhead.

Jess smiled at Avril.

'Are you Ok?' Avril asked her ' the bathroom's free.'

Jess blushed and Nate gave her a hug. Jess removed the test from her bag and went to the bathroom. As she waited for the result, Avril put the kettle on again and Nate stood in the doorframe nervously picking at his thumb. Sophie came downstairs and to the front door in her *Lipsy* tracksuit and white trainers. Her skin was the colour of a tangerine with fake tan.

'I'm going out.' She shouted as she made to open the door.

'Not until you've washed that off.' Avril shouted from the kitchen.

'Mum!' countered Sophie ' I'm twelve, everyone's wearing it.'

'Sophie! Wash it off and then you can go out" Avril's tone held a warning that Sophie knew to heed 'if not you're grounded'.

Avril had had this fight before. Not yet a teenager but acting like she was. Avril knew that this was the time that the reins had to stay tight. She didn't want Sophie going off the rails. Sophie tutted but headed back upstairs defeated. The downstairs bathroom door opened. Avril poured the water into three waiting mugs. Whatever the outcome a cup of tea would be welcomed. She finished making the tea, put the mugs on a tray and carried it into the living room. Nate and Jess were parting from a hug. They both had a wide smile. ' Mum,' Nate said ' you're going to be a granny…one day, but not right now.'

'False alarm' added Jess.

Avril let out a sigh as she smiled.

'Tea?' she asked as they all took a breath.

Pittenweem   June 2021

CHAPTER TWENTY - SEVEN

' and when I got to the shore she was sitting on the bus which was moving away and her mum was waving her off. ' Davy finished.

Maybeth put down her fork. She had just finished scooping the last of the peas from her plate into her mouth. She took a minute to chew and swallow them.

'and you never saw her again?' she asked.

'No,' Davy flushed ' but, I wish now I had spoken to her mum that day or gone to see her after. I wish I had told her everything.'

' This place is tiny. Is her mum still here?' Maybeth asked.

'I still see her round and about but I keep myself to myself. I think I've just been too afraid to be around people in case I hear something I don't want to hear. I'm not much of a one for the gossip.'

Maybeth nodded. She could bet that this was the most conversation this man had had in a long time. She didn't want it to dry up so she carried on.

' So, tell me about you.'

Davy looked startled. 'Me?' he chuckled. She liked his laugh. It was a rich and throaty laugh. Rugged, like the man himself. He had a twinkle in his eyes too. He looked happy.

'Well,' he continued ' I live on my own at the end of the harbour. When I'm not on the boats I like to fish and watch rugby. I like watching documentaries about arctic animals and I don't like noisy music.' He smiled. ' That's about me, I think. Your turn.'

Maybeth returned the smile and told Davy about her life down South. She told him about her adoptive parents, Laura and her work, her friends and her love of rugby too. ' We should catch a game.' Davy suggested. 'If you would like to?' he added feeling that he may be rushing into things for her. He was this woman's dad and he now didn't want her out of his life.

'I'd love that,' Maybeth answered enthusiastically ' I've just signed off on the house that I was selling and I am officially on holiday for 2 weeks. I can do what I want for the first time in a very long time.'

Debbie had come over to collect the plates.

'So, the holiday has started now Maybeth. You've sold that house, I wish we could open the champers. 'Damn Covid,' she grumbled.

' I've got a bottle of Moet et Chandon in the fridge. It's been just waiting for a special occasion too.'

Debbie shook her head morosely. With the pandemic, the usual rush of engagement dinners and hen-do starter meals had been cancelled or postponed. She was desperate to be able to celebrate something again.

' We'll need to make do with fizzy apple then.' She sighed and went to collect the juice and three champagne flutes. As Debbie handed over the glasses, Maybeth looked again at the man who was her father. He was the route to the rest of her bloodline. She had many questions she needed answers to, but she had time now. Debbie raised her glass, encouraging the other two to do the same.

'To the future!' Debbie toasted.

'To the future!' they cheerfully responded.

Pittenweem   August 2018

CHAPTER TWENTY – EIGHT

Julie McKay opened the door to the restaurant and immediately saw the balloons. 'Happy Retirement' banners bedecked the walls and people smiled and cheered as she entered. Her friends from the golf club had organized a 'wee do'. She looked around and saw not only her colleagues but her family too. There was her sister Morag, her cousins Lawrence and Jim and there was Avril. Avril had come too. Julie took a breath. Things had always been difficult with Avril. She had left home so young and had never really come home. In fact, now that she thought about it, Julie couldn't remember Avril ever coming back. They had always met up outside of the harbour town. Julie would go up to the City or they would meet at the nearby beaches with her grandchildren. Avril had not set foot in the old house since she had left at seventeen.

'Gran!' a voice boomed, breaking her from her memories and attaching her back into the pleasant present. There he was. Her big boy. Her grandson. Nathaniel stood in front of her and lifted her off the ground in a firm but gentle hug. He now stood an easy six foot. She loved her grandchildren. Since Nathaniel had passed his driving test he was a frequent visitor. He brought Sophie with him on the occasions that he could. Avril had no problem with the kids coming, but why had she never visited?

Was this really the first time she had looked at this in any depth? She brushed the thought away as Avril approached her.

'Happy Retirement Mum.' Avril kissed her mum's powdery cheek. She had always smelled of powder. She must still be using the same make as she did when Avril had been a child. The peach scent was so familiar and Avril had to step slightly back as she felt her eyes water with emotion. She gave her mum a smile.

'Thanks Love.' Julie replied returning the smile and giving Avril's hand a squeeze.

The Head waiter briskly ushered them all to the tables and soon the chatter and laughter filled the space. Sophie regaled everyone with her terrible dating stories, how boys were maddening and gave a quick make up tutorial to anyone who was listening to her. Julie watched as her friends and family mingled easily. Nate and Jess looking at Gareth the greenkeepers phone. Probably helping him to fix something. He wasn't very technical when it came to phones and was always asking Julie to help him with messages and updates at work. Sophie talking to anyone who would listen and Avril and her dad in deep conversation and looking at photos of Ronnie's latest hobby. Gardening. Ronnie was enjoying learning about new plants on his phone. Learning about different soils and seasonal planting. Julie wasn't as keen, but she listened while he happily chattered, passing on his new knowledge to her.

Julie's eyes filled with tears. She felt someone take her hand and looked to her side.

' You OK, sis?' Morag asked.

Julie smiled and nodded at her little sister. Her chilled, laid - back sister. Morag, who from a very early aged had enjoyed nature and creativity and bohemian floaty clothing. Morag who always had the wild carefree nature and had left when she could to pursue her love of Art. This was who Avril took after.

' It's a lovely party. It's good seeing everyone together again' she paused before adding ' did you ever wonder why Avril never came back to visit?'

Morag sighed. ' I did, often.'

They both looked over at Avril who had now been joined by Nate who had taken the phone and was scrolling through the phone looking impressed at what he was seeing. Ronnie was grinning proudly by his other side.

' I should have been there more ' Julie whispered almost to herself.

' I don't think it was you she was running away from' Morag whispered back ' perhaps one day she'll tell us.'

Morag gave Julie's hand a quick squeeze and let go.

' Perhaps' Julie answered.

Pittenweem July 2021

CHAPTER TWENTY – NINE

The kettle had just switched itself off when the knock at the door came.

'Come in!' shouted Julie 'It's open.'

Julie peeked her head out of the kitchen door into the hallway to see who was coming in through the front door. It was a man she didn't recognize. No, hold on. It was a man she didn't recognise but a boy she'd known well.

'Davy McCreath?' she said in wonder.

Davy came towards her with the same nervous smile he'd always given around adults. He was now a man in his late forties. He would be fifty next year.

'I wasn't sure that this was the house.' He whispered.

'Well. if it's me you're looking for, you're at the right house'.

Julie and Ronnie had sold the family home at the harbour three years ago. The house was historical and a listed building, so they had sold it to be made into luxury guest rooms. It has been stripped back to the bare brick the way it had been when it was a chandlery. The guest rooms were proving very popular. Julie and Ronnie had got a good price and had bought this new build with a garden further up the hill. The views out to sea were breathtaking and at least now they were sheltered from the haar that hit them from the harbourside on chillier days.

Julie didn't miss the sea salty swirl of the wind catching in her throat as she tried to lock the front door and quickly get to her car on the way out. This had been a good investment and at their age, having a garden to potter about in was nice. Ronnie had retired too and Nate and Jess had a baby on the way, so Julie was looking forward to the Great Granny garden time.

' You look as if you've seen a ghost, son. Are you OK? ' Julie asked

'Take a seat.' She indicated to one of a chair round a small glass dining table. Davy sat. 'Thanks'.

'Tea or Coffee?' Julie asked.

'Coffee please' He answered taking off his cap and laying it on his lap 'but only if it's not too much bother.'

Julie made small talk about the weather and the garden while she prepared Davy's coffee. She put the mug down on a puffin coaster on the table in front and then gave him the friends preparation. The milk carton and the sugar bag and a teaspoon. Davy added the sugar. Four heaped teaspoons and a small amount of milk and stirred it noisily, tapping the back of the spoon on the rim of the mug twice when he had finished. He then handed the spoon to Julie who put it in the sink.

'So,' she said as she sat opposite Davy cradling her own mug 'What can I do for you?'

Davy looked at his mug, sighed and started to speak.

'I need to take you back to 1993...'

Edinburgh   June 2013

CHAPTER THIRTY

Sophie was sitting on the stool in front of the T.V. Avril was braiding her hair. Sophie had already applied her fake tan and her make-up and once Avril had finished she would be putting on the bridesmaids dress. Chris was getting married again. Sophie was the only bridesmaid and Nate was his best man. Avril was looking forward to a night out with her friends from work but would wait until Sophie and Nate had gone before getting ready. Sophie chattered on nervously about her excitement for the day ahead as Avril finished the braiding. She was so proud of her children. Nate was now at Uni doing his degree and Sophie was fifteen and doing well in school. She really wanted to do a beauty course and run her own business. She could as well. She had a good business brain and loved people. She was such a confident girl.

'OK, all done' Avril said as she put the brush down on the arm of the nearest chair.

'Thanks mum' Sophie grinned, leaping up and checking herself in the mirror over the fireplace. She left the living room and rushed upstairs to get into the dress. Avril smiled and shook her head. Where did she get the energy? Avril had remembered running as a child. She loved taking part in the long-distance running races at school. Nate had never really shown much aptitude for racing, but Sophie was fast. A track runner, her PE teacher had said at the last parents evening. The parents evening that Chris couldn't make because he was moving wife number two out and wife number three in. It was sad the way things had happened, but Chris just didn't seem to have any stickability. Sophie and Nate were older now and seemed to take it all in their stride, but second wife Melanie had had a baby. Joel. He was three. The age Sophie had been when Chris had up and left them.

Nate appeared in the doorway. All kilted and handsome.

'Is she ready yet?" he asked his mum, pointing up the stairs.

'Yes, she is!' Sophie shouted down as she carefully made her way down. She looked stunning in a silver coloured dress with a lemon and silver shawl with heeled sandals in matching shades.

'My beautiful babies.' Avril gasped as Nate held his arm out for his little sister. 'Have a great time' she gulped.

' We won't' said Sophie

Avril gave her a look.

'I'm only joking, but I'm never doing this again' she giggled.

' Well I might for you.' She added quickly.

'Don't hold your breath' answered Avril ' now go or you'll be late.'

'Love you' They shouted as they left the house.

'Love you back' she answered and watched them go.

Pittenweem   July 2021

CHAPTER THIRTY – ONE

Julie sat in a stunned silence. How could she have missed a whole pregnancy? How could she not have seen? Why hadn't Avril confided in her? What sort of mother had she been that her only daughter couldn't come to her? The baby was now 29. The baby was in Pittenweem. Staying at their old house, or part of their old house. She was possibly in the same room where her own mother had slept. Definitely in a room her own mother had played in. Maybeth. She liked that name. Julie's daughter had given another person a name. A life. Julie put her head in her hands. What should she do? She would have to move slowly. If she phoned Avril now this could do damage. Would Avril want to know? Had she ever thought about the baby? Of course, she had. Julie mused. That's why she had gone. This place was too much of a reminder. She had to tell Ronnie. She opened the kitchen door into the garden and called to him. He was in the garden shed, where he had been making a bird box. He couldn't hear her over the noise of his hammering. She went out into the garden and called him again. This time the hammer stopped he appeared at the shed door.

'Can I borrow you for a minute?' she asked.

'Aye, what is it?' he answered.

'I'll wait until you've sat down' she said, moving back into the kitchen and refilling the kettle.

Cap Salou, Spain   June 2018

CHAPTER THIRTY - TWO

Avril was enjoying the peace. Sophie had decided that they needed a holiday, so they had booked flights to Spain. It was 6.30 in the morning and Avril was sitting on the balcony of their third-floor apartment looking out on to the calm Balearic sea. It was beautiful. The sun was casting a watery shadow onto the sea which made it sparkle dully, but the colours were still amazing light blues merging with pale yellow and silver. Avril had never been abroad before and in the two days they had been here she had enjoyed the heat of the sun, the chatter of the locals in a language unfamiliar to her and the cars driving on the wrong side of the road. This early in the morning she could hear slight traffic noises, the clattering in the hotel kitchen as breakfast was being prepared and the occasional chirp of a bird in the trees slightly below.

They were going to a theme park today. Sophie had decided they would have day about choosing the activities. Avril's activity yesterday had been a day at the beach. It had been very relaxing. Sophie had gone for a run and Avril had sat with the new *Jojo Moyes* book. Sophie had swum in the sea; Avril had baked on the sand. Bliss. They had found a little taberna and had fish and chips before returning to the hotel for a shower and a change of clothes. They had then taken in some of the hotels entertainment. A man with eight parrots that did tricks. It was quite amusing but the birds looked bored.

Avril took her phone out of her dressing gown pocket and turned it on. Eight missed calls from Nate. The last one had been at 3am. Something bad must have happened. She didn't hesitate in pressing the call button After three rings Nate picked up, 'Mum' he said frantically.

'What's happened?' Avril said at the same time.

'It's Jess, she's in hospital' he managed before bursting into tears.

'OK, why is she in hospital, Nathaniel ?' Avril always called him by his full name when the situation was serious.

' A car crashed into hers and she had to be cut out.'

Avril closed her eyes.

'Is she OK?'

'I don't know" Nate answered quietly. ' I can't lose her, Mum.'

He broke into more sobs.

'I'm coming home.' Avril decided, standing up and heading for her bedroom to pack.

'No!' Nate said definitely. 'You are not. I'll call you when I know what's happening here. I'm at the hospital. There is nothing you can do. If anything, ... changes" she heard him gulp ' I'll let you know.'

'What exactly happened?' Avril asked, sitting down on the bed.

Nate explained that Jess had been travelling down a long stretch of road at, what the police had told him, was a normal speed, when a car had come out of a side entrance at speed and hit her passenger side with such force that her car had hit a railing on the driver's side across the road. It was ten o'clock at night. Jess had been knocked unconscious but had come round before the ambulance had arrived. They seemed to think there had been a crushing injury but by the time Nate had been contacted by Jess's mum and she and her dad had arrived at the hospital she had been taken into emergency and right now Nate and Jess's parents were in the waiting area. A nurse had kept them up to date and although they didn't think the injuries were life threatening they had to err on the side of caution and look out for any internal bleeding or adverse brain activity. Nate sounded exhausted Avril thought. Poor Jess. She was just like another daughter to Avril. She and Nate had got engaged at Christmastime and the wedding was all planned for New Years Eve this year. Six months away. She hoped Jess would be OK. She realized the phone had gone silent.

'Nate?' she said

'I'll go now, Mum' he yawned. 'I'm going to try and get some sleep.'

'OK son. Keep me up to date.'

'Will do.' He said quietly. Love you.'

'Love you both too.' She answered as the line went dead. She sat cradling the silent phone as Sophie's tousled head and half shut face appeared in the doorway.

' I heard chatting .' she said grumpily as she threw herself on to Avril's bed.

'It was Nate. Jess is in hospital.' Avril told her.

'Why? How?' Sophie jumped up.

Avril put her hands on Sophie's arm.

' I'll explain when you take a breath and sit back down.'

Sophie was always so dramatic and Jess and her adored each other. Sophie's eyes started to glisten.

'Soph, she's going to be Ok.' Avril heard herself praying in her gut that this was the case.

'Come here' she said, brushing Sophie into a hug.

'It's all going to be fine.'

Pittenweem   July 2021

CHAPTER THIRTY – THREE

Maybeth watched from the window. She had been sitting in her room all morning. Yesterday had been an emotional one. She had met the man who had fathered her. She now knew her mother's name, her mother's age and a fair bit about her background. That poor girl must have been so frightened. The feelings of abandonment that had begun to claw at her since she had made the decision to look for her mother had started to dissipate. Her father seemed like a nice, quiet man. Uncomplicated and gentle. He had revealed that he had never married because he was married to his work. He was a daily fisherman. He had worked the waters around the East Coast since his fourteenth birthday. The boat Maybeth had seen on the harbour, The *Betty Smith,* was his old one. He had been a boatsman, or boats boy on it when it had come here new in 1993. The year, Maybeth was born. Davy had bought it a couple of years ago to fix up. The purchase had been a heart buy with the date having links to the year his life changed forever. Maybeth had been taken aback by this revelation and she felt tears start to form behind her eyes. These people she had met were so kind. Davy had known about her for her whole life and had never been able to do anything about finding her through fear of rejection and thick red tape.

As they had chatted yesterday he seemed to relax and loose the tension in his shoulder and neck. His eyes appeared to twinkle more too. Maybeth had left around six and returned to her rooms. The rooms, he had told her, where her mother Avril had once lived with her mum and dad. She didn't believe in luck or fate she just thought it was about coincidence.

Maybeth had phoned Laura and told her everything she had heard. Laura was excited and had wanted every detail gone over at least half a dozen times. It had taken Maybeth a long time to finish that call and then she had called her Mum and Dad. Ellen and Sid had always encouraged her, and did so still. They had given her the security and love she needed to make her the adult she had become. Sure, there had been teenage fights but Ellen and Sid had never given up on her. She felt a sudden flash of something at the thought. She had been given up on but the thought reduced to nothing when the picture of a certain happy and relieved fisherman came back into her thoughts. She had decided to have a lazy morning. Davy had said he was going to tell Avril's parents. Julie and Ronnie, her maternal grandparents, who to Davy's knowledge, until now had never known she existed. He said that he was pretty sure that if Julie had known she would have been asking questions over the years. He also felt pretty sure, knowing Julie's nature that she would have led the search to find her granddaughter and never given up.

Her paternal grandparents had died and her aunt, Davy's twin, Davina, had passed away due to cancer in her spine only last year.

' She would have loved you.' Davy had said, tearfully.

Maybeth finished her conversation with Ellen and with a sigh moved from the window. She had made arrangements to meet up with Davy at teatime or 5pm dinnertime as she called it. She moved to the kitchen, switched on the TV and checked the Netflix channel for a film to watch,. *Notting Hill* was there, her favourite. She made herself a cup of tea, opened a packet of ginger biscuits and settled down with Hugh and Julia for a few hours relaxation.

Edinburgh, New Year   2018

CHAPTER THIRTY – FOUR

Nate stood at the altar waiting nervously for Jess to arrive. The past six months had been fraught with worry as to whether the wedding would go ahead. Jess was having to take things very slowly with her mobility. She had suffered a broken pelvis and had been in traction for a month. She still used a wheelchair but was beginning to walk using sticks. Today, she was being wheeled down the aisle halfway and would walk the last part with her father on one arm and her brother on the other. The music started and the minister spoke to Nate quietly, giving him instruction and calming his nerves. Jess and Nate were not particularly religious but with the amount of church wedding photography bookings Nate had worked, he had struck up a friendship with this minister and he had offered to marry them. At a nod from the minister Nate turned around to see Jess coming towards him on her father's arm. Sophie was wheeling the empty wheelchair which was bedecked with flowers to match the brides bouquet, which was, at this moment being held, rather reverently by her sweating brother in fear that he would crush or drop them. Sophie had lain her own bouquet in the wheelchair. As they reached the front of the church at the altar, Sophie removed her bouquets and Jess sat back down. She looked beautiful in a one shouldered Grecian gown in ivory and a wreath of flowers in her hair. Miniature white roses and cala lily. Nate beamed at her and leant down to squeeze her hand.

From her pew, Avril watched lovingly. These two really meant the world to her. Jess was such a strong young woman and Nate doted on her. Standing beside Nate, and his best man, was his half-brother, Joel. Now nine. Nate had asked him to be a groomsman or usher. Joel was a shy boy but Nate brought the best out in him. Joel worshipped his brother and sister. Nate was now whispering to Jess as the minister spoke about marriage being the union of two people and those joined together should have no man put them asunder. This made Avril look at Chris. He was looking old. His hair was greying at the sides and he had bags under his eyes. Her must have felt her looking because he turned to catch her looking and gave her a small smile. She smiled back and returned her gaze to her son and nearly daughter-in-law.

The service was beautiful and very personal to the couple. The reception took place in a converted barn just outside of the town. Another happy client had offered her services and her venue. The meal had finished. Rough farmhouse pate slabs served with warm sourdough toast and cherry chutney or tomato salad to start. Braised beef and vegetables, Monkfish risotto or stuffed peppers for the main and crème brulee or fruit medley for dessert. There had been wine to match with every dish and Avril was feeling a little bit tired. She was sitting at the table with Sophie and her parents watching her Aunty Morag who was encouraging people to come and have their pictures taken. Avril felt content. She was happy today. Happy and blessed. The evening festivities carried on but Avril said her goodbyes just before eleven o'clock. She had lasted longer than she thought she would. Something had felt wrong for the past few weeks. She seemed to be tired a lot. She put it down to the stress of the wedding planning but she had decided to get herself checked and had an appointment for next Wednesday to see the Doctor. Avril shared a taxi with her Aunty Morag who was dozing lightly beside her. Aunty Morag was staying overnight with her. She loved her and had confided in her a lot over the years. She had told her all her secrets. Well...almost all of them. Avril looked out of the window and gently nudged Morag awake as the taxi pulled up at the door. Maybe tomorrow she would tell her everything.

Pittenweem   July 2021

CHAPTER THIRTY-FIVE

Maybeth walked into the café and looked around for Davy. They had agreed to meet at five and it was just leaving quarter to. She was always a bit early. For everything.

'He's not here yet' Debbie shouted over the noise of the coffee machine.

Debbie was enjoying this fact finding mission and loved the mystery. She and

Maybeth had become quite friendly. Maybeth really liked Debbie's enthusiasm and lust for life. She had a real get-it-done attitude, Maybeth sat down and took off her jacket. She was feeling a little nervous. Had Davy met up with her grandparents and told them about her? As she was putting her jacket over the chair she felt someone joining her at the table. She turned and her smiling father was sitting across from her. He was still wearing his mask but she couldn't mistake the crinkling at the corner of his eyes. He was definitely smiling.

'Good evening' he said cheerfully. Maybeth smiled back quizzically.

'What's all the smiling for?' she asked.

'What? ' Davy answered, laughing 'can't a father who has just been reunited with his daughter have a happy face?'

Maybeth smiled some more ' Of course.' She replied then she added seriously ' did you see my grandmother?'

Davy continued smiling and took off his mask.

'That I did.' He said ' and she was totally unaware of everything.'

Maybeth's expression changed from easy smile to one of reflection.

' I thought that might be the case' she said solemnly. 'Was she angry?'

'Not in the slightest,' Davy answered ' she was curious about you, very surprised that she hadn't noticed, a little bit upset with Avril for not telling her but I never detected any anger. No.' Maybeth nodded. Davy went on. ' She always wondered why Avril never came back.'

'Never?' asked Maybeth.

'Never.' Answered Davy. ' She would meet her mum and dad in the city for visits but has never been back here.'

'Wow' said Maybeth.

'However,' continued Davy, ' she did say her son and daughter visit often.'

Maybeth caught her breath. She had siblings. A half sister and a half brother. She looked at Davy who seemed a bit sad as he said it. Could it be possible that he still loved her mother? Probably, she thought. He had never married. She started to feel a bit sorry for him then.

' A son and a daughter.' She repeated.

At that moment Debbie came over to take the order. Maybeth chose steak pie, potatoes and carrots and Davy, the battered haddock, chips and mushy peas.

'You'd think I'd be fed up with fish' he smiled as he returned the menu to the holder.

There was a slight lull in the conversation as Davy let Maybeth process what he had told her. Then, tentatively, she asked

' Does my grandmother want to meet me?'

Davy nodded slowly.

' She does, but only if you want to meet her.'

Maybeth nodded back. ' I do.'

They chatted on until the food arrived and when they had empty mouths and empty plates they chatted on some more. Davy was a funny man with hilarious stories from the sea. Maybeth was enchanted by this big man who was half her. She had some funny tales too and as Debbie looked on she could see the resemblance in the way they both used their hands to tell their stories and had the ease in the way they spoke to each other. This was lovely to watch and she felt quite honoured that she was part of this story. Maybeth and Davy had filled her in on everything so far. She felt like part of the family too.

After a while and a cup of tea, Maybeth yawned and put her jacket on. It was still early evening, but she felt sleepy all of a sudden.

'Do you want to come to mine for a coffee?' Davy asked.

'I would like that very much.' Maybeth replied.

'I've got photos of your grandparents on my side and your Aunty Davina, if you want to see them.'

Maybeth suddenly brightened up.

'That would be amazing.'

She stood up and picked up her bag. She settled the bill after a small argument about who was paying, she was stubborn and she could now see where it came from, but, she won and they then said goodbye to Debbie.

' See you both tomorrow and I want all the details.' She shouted after them as they exited.

Tomorrow Maybeth would meet her maternal grandparents but for tonight she was going to see the other ones.

Edinburgh Jan 2019

CHAPTER THIRTY-SIX

Avril didn't like this part of the hospital administration form. How many children do you have? It had that question on the form. She always ticked three but with that tick or cross, came a pain and an urge to cry. She handed the form back to the waiting nurse and continued to sit and wait in her chair. She had had two lots of blood tests done and one had come back showing low blood platelets. This appointment was to see a specialist who would hopefully tell her what was wrong. Apart from the fatigue she felt fine. It just seemed to wash over her at times and make her want to curl up into a ball and go to sleep. She opened a book she had brought with her and began to read. She got four pages in and was just starting to enjoy it. (A tale of a dysfunctional family with a little boy who ate grass and two daughters who were trying to find a way to escape the madness). When her name was called, Avril stood up and headed towards a smiling young doctor who immediately put her at her ease as he reminded her so much of Nate.

The doctor welcomed her into his consulting room and pointed her to the seat on the opposite side of his desk. After a few pleasantries and a check on her date of birth and to see whether or not she was a Miss, a Ms or a Mrs, the doctor looked Avril in the eye.

'OK,' the doctor began ' we have looked at all the bloodwork and we are pretty sure that you are in an early menopause.

Avril looked at the doctor in puzzlement. 'Is that all?' she asked letting out a small laugh.

'It looks like it but I still want to run an MRI scan and an ultrasound on you just to be very certain.' The doctor looked at Avril's notes and moved slightly in his seat.

'We had looked for the markers of immuno-deficiency diseases but they all came back clear, so it's early menopause. You're 42 and menopause usually hits round about mid-50s. You said "is that all" but some women suffer some terrible symptoms. I'll give you some leaflets to look at and there are some terrific websites which help with information and we have some hospital forums too.

Avril wanted to hug this man. She had been worried that it was something serious and deadly and that she would die without seeing her baby again. As she stood to shake the doctor's outstretched hand and leave, she vowed that from now she would do all that she could to find her daughter.

Pittenweem   July 2021

CHAPTER THIRTY-SEVEN

'Julie, you are going to wear that flooring away to toothpicks' Ronnie laughed as he sat on the sofa and watched his wife pace back and forward in front of the kitchen window across the wooden flooring. Julie had been up since five o'clock in the morning cleaning and polishing her already spotless house. It was now two in the afternoon.

'Ronnie, what if she blames us?' Julie fretted.

'She's not going to blame us.'

' How could Avril have kept this to herself?' Julie groaned. ' How could we not have noticed?'

Ronnie stood up and went to her. Taking her into a hug he sighed gently. 'It's going to be OK'.

They stood together for a minute and drew apart when they heard the doorbell ring. Julie gasped and gripped Ronnie's wrist.

' I feel sick.' She said.

'You sit down and I'll get the door' Ronnie said.

Julie sat down, her heart beating loudly in her chest. Ronnie left the room and Julie tried to calm herself down.

Maybeth waited for the door to open. She was fueled by a mixture of excitement and apprehension. Maybe this was too much too soon. A few weeks ago she didn't know about any of these people, had had no inclination or desire to know about them. Now though, the curiosity had been too much, and she now hoped that she wasn't to become the cat that curiosity killed.

The door opened and a kind man stood with a wide smile and happy sparkling eyes. Eyes the same colour as her own. They looked at each other for a few beats before Ronnie remembered where he was. She was so like Avril. His little girl who he had been sad for when she went away, but also proud of as she achieved so much in her life. Ronnie and Julie had lived in Pittenweem all of their lives. They had both been lucky and when Ronnie had stopped working the boats due to an argument with his boss he had found a great job in the library and registrars office. This girl standing before him had never come to be registered in his office. He felt a thickness in his throat and cleared it.

'Welcome' he said to Maybeth 'come on in.'

'Thank you so much.' Maybeth answered in her soft London burr.

As they entered the living room, Julie rushed forward and without thinking, put her arms out and hugged Maybeth. Maybeth was slightly startled. She had just got used to not being able to hug her parents and friends down south but she recovered and returned the embrace.

'We didn't know' Julie rushed out. ' we would have helped to raise you if we'd have known.'

Maybeth nodded, she understood the woman's need to be seen as non - complicit in this too.

'Please, sit down and I'll make us all some tea.' Ronnie offered, feeling the strength of the emotion in the room. Julie reluctantly let go of Maybeth. This was her flesh and blood and looked so much like Avril and Davy. Maybeth sat at a distance from where Julie was sitting, sticking to at least,, some of the rules. Julie's heart was still hammering. This girl was beautiful, This Maybeth, her granddaughter.

'I'm sorry' Julie said ' I just had to know you were real, it's all been ...'

'Very quick?' continued Maybeth. 'I know, I'm sorry if it's been a shock. I didn't know anything until Davy spotted me in my car. Imagine if I'd left earlier or later.'

'Well, I'm so glad he saw you.' Julie said.

Ronnie appeared from the kitchen with a pre-arranged tea tray. Julie had been meticulous in the planning. Three teacups with saucers from their wedding china fifty three years ago. A bowl containing sugar, a box of sweeteners in case Maybeth preferred them, a jug of milk and a jug of cream, a cafetière and a teapot of English Breakfast tea and some good quality biscuits.

Maybeth poured herself some tea and watched as Ronnie worked his way round the cafetiere before giving up and pouring himself some tea. She stifled a smile, but really warmed to the man as he muddled through muttering and laughing as he went. Julie, Maybeth noticed didn't have any tea or coffee, but instead, sipped on a small glass of water.

'So,' said Ronnie as he sat down finally with his tea beside his wife

'tell us about yourself.'

For two hours Maybeth talked easily with her grandparents. The nerves she had felt had disappeared. They were all puzzled as to why Avril had felt the need to hide her pregnancy, but, going back to that time and in this small town it could have been very difficult for her. There were tears and some sadness as Julie and Ronnie filled Maybeth in about her mother. Sadness that they all had missed out on so much time. There was laughter too when Ronnie spoke about Maybeth's siblings. Maybeth had noticed photographs on the walls. Baby photographs, photographs of children on beaches, on bikes, in sandpits, pre-teens with thumbs up, teenagers with baseball caps and attitude, a wedding photograph, the bride in a wheelchair grinning happily as the groom and a bridesmaid bend down on either side. Nate and Sophie. After the chat Maybeth felt like she knew these people too. There was definitely a resemblance.

' I think it's time.' Julie said after the tea had been replenished and they had become more relaxed.

'I think so too.' Ronnie agreed.

'Time for what?' Maybeth asked.

' To call your mother.' Julie replied.

Edinburgh July 2021

CHAPTER THIRTY-EIGHT

Avril had just finished putting the shopping away when she heard the phone. It was her mum calling. She sat down in the big comfortable sofa and brought her knees up under her. She could be on the phone for hours with her mum. If her dad had bought a new type of plant for the garden she would hear all about it. She now knew what a perennial and a hardy annual were. Julie would want to know all about Nate and Sophie. She loved her grandchildren and could spend a whole call just talking about them. Avril pressed the answer button on the phone.

'Hi Mum' she said. There was a pause on the other end.

'Hi, Mum' Avril repeated

'Avril' her mum answered slowly.

Avril felt something hit the bottom of her stomach. Something was wrong. This call was different. She immediately thought of her dad. What if something terrible had happened.

'Is everything Ok? Is Dad ok?'

'Yes, we're both fine, we've got a visitor love.'

'Oh right'. She was pretty sure Nate and Jess had a hospital appointment and Sophie was working.

'Anyone I know?' she ventured, her thoughts turning but trying to remain upbeat.

'Yes, I would think so.' Julie answered.

Avril closed her eyes. Why all the guesswork? She shook her head and opened her eyes again.

'OK Mum, I give up. Who is your visitor?'

She heard Julie take a deep breath before she answered.

'Maybeth'

There was a long moment of silence as Avril processed what she had just heard.

'Did you really say Maybeth?' Avril whispered into the phone as if saying it loudly would make her disappear.

'I did love,' Julie whispered back holding back the tears for the years that her daughter must have wept alone.

'Is…Is she Ok?' Avril could feel her own tears coming. Her eldest daughter was sitting in her mother's house. How had that happened? How long had her mother known? She needed to find out.

'There's so much to talk about.' said Julie. ' can you come here?'

'I'm on my way' Avril said, then added ' does she want to see me?'

'Do you want to talk to her?'

Avril gulped in a breath.

'Does she want to talk to me? Mum I'm going to cry. It's a lot to take in.'

Avril heard Julie talking to someone in the room and the phone was passed.

'Hello, Avril?' a young voice asked.

'Maybeth?' Avril whispered. 'Is that really you?'

'It's really me.' Maybeth laughed softly. ' I know this will be difficult for you to take in but I'd really like to meet you. If you want to? There's no pressure? Maybeth finished, secretly hoping that she hadn't given Avril an easy out. She heard a sob coming from the other end of the phone and could feel tears building inside herself.

'I'd like that very much.' Avril answered. ' Will you still be there tomorrow, or I could drive over tonight?'

"I'll be here tomorrow. I'm here for another week and then I'm heading home.'

Home. Avril wondered where home was for Maybeth.

'OK, I'll be there first thing tomorrow. I'm so happy that you're there.' Avril gulped.

'I'll see you tomorrow, Mum' Maybeth answered as she handed the phone back to Julie. Maybeth felt a rush of something, she wasn't sure what, excitement, love or anticipation knowing that she was going to meet her birth mother in the morning.

Julie said goodbye to Avril. There would be questions for Avril to answer to her mother too, but, this evening would be the time to let Avril get her head round the reality that her daughter, the daughter she had pined for, was alive and well and sitting in her mother's living room. As Avril sat in a daze the door opened and Nate and Jess walked in. Nate noticed at once that she had been crying.

'What's happened?' he asked.

Avril looked up at Nate and smiled.

'Maybeth is at your gran's house.'

Nate stopped and stared wide mouthed at Avril. He had known about Maybeth for so long and she had been spoken about freely by Sophie and Avril, but, in keeping with Avril's wishes Gran and

Grandad were not to know until Maybeth made contact. Avril did not want her parents upset. This had been hard for Sophie, but she had managed it during her late childhood by pretending she had an imaginary friend called Mary in case she slipped up. Now it hit Nate. His big sister was now a real person who had found her family. Nate walked over to his mum and put his hands out to her. She took them and stood up. Nate twirled her around the room, whooping happily like a schoolboy. Jess looked on laughing too. Then Avril stooped and fell down onto the sofa again. Nate sat opposite her in the armchair and Jess flopped down beside Avril.

' Your gran and grandad didn't know anything.' Avril said trying to catch her breath.

Nate looked at her. ' You asked us not to say. So, we didn't.'

Avril put her head in her hands.

'It was just a terrible time and I feel really bad, but I just had to get away…' the words were tumbling unbidden now as if a dam had burst open.

'… and I didn't want to say because it would get them upset and I couldn't find Maybeth and didn't know where to look and… ' Avril stopped talking and wept.

Nate swapped seats with Jess and put his arms around Avril.

' It's alright mum.' He soothed.

'She's found you now' Jess added ' Its all going to be fine.'

Avril looked up and smiled at Jess through her tears. She could feel her hair wet against her cheek. Nate smoothed it away and hugged her. Avril snuggled into her big son and bit at a hangnail on her thumb. She always did this when she was worried.

'I'm going tomorrow morning.'

'Do you want a lift?' Nate asked grinning. ' I'm off tomorrow and I want to come and support you and meet the person who has taken up a lot of my mother's thinking time over the years.'

Avril looked at Nate now who had moved himself over to the armchair and was perched on the arm smoothing Jess's hair lovingly.

Nate continued.

' I remember how sad you looked sometimes after you told us about Maybeth. I wonder how she found us.'

'I don't know, but something took her to your gran's. We'll find out tomorrow.'

'What time does Sophie finish?' Jess asked.

'Seven' replied Avril.

'She's going to be so excited.' Nate giggled. ' You'll have to scrape her off the ceiling.'

'She'll want to go too.' Jess said matter-of-factly.

'We're all going' Nate said, kissing Jess tenderly.

Jess smiled at him. This kind, sweet man. Since her accident she had had to rebuild up her strength and over the years she had learned to walk with only the occasional wince. Jess now used a stick and her self confidence had taken a real battering, but, Nate had always been there for her. She had felt so guilty and that she was holding him back from living his life. Nate was full of love and re-assurances. Avril was a good mum and had always encouraged Jess too. She deserved this peace. Jess had helped Avril to search but it was very difficult. They had found two Maybeth's but then Avril had got cold feet and didn't want to hurt the Maybeth who may now have been adopted, or didn't want to know anything about the woman who had abandoned her.

It had been horrible to watch Avril's face change when programmes about lost babies came on the T.V.

'I've just had a thought.' Nate said, breaking into Jess's reverie 'are we all allowed to be there?'

'We can be as long as we wear masks and stay distanced. Avril responded.

'That's going to be hard.' Nate added ' You'll want a hug.'

Avril bit her lip. She desperately wanted to hold her baby in her arms.

She had always longed for it, imagined it and tomorrow, although no longer a baby, but, then again, always her baby, she hoped Maybeth would let her hug her.

'Why don't we run you and let you go in and we can come later?' Nate said.

'No!" Avril started.

'Mum' Nate pushed on ' I think you need time with Maybeth first and I'm still a bit freaked by too many people.'

Nate had always had a sensible, practical head. He knew Avril hadn't ever been back to her birth town and he also knew she didn't like driving long distance. They were only fifty one miles from Pittenweem but that would seem too long, especially with the thoughts that would be going through Avril's mind.

'I think you might be right' Avril agreed 'as always.'

Nate grinned. ' Now, who wants a cuppa?' He asked, springing to his feet.

Edinburgh July 2021

CHAPTER THIRTY – NINE

Avril paced the kitchen floor. It was just gone seven in the morning. She had seen nearly every hour on the clock through the night and her stomach was churning with nerves. Sophie had got in just before eight o'clock last night and she had told her about Maybeth. As Nate had predicted she *was* excited. She had actually done a lap of the garden, screaming with joy.

Avril had laughed with her. This was the reaction that she had felt too, but, she didn't want to get too excited. She wanted to apologise. The guilt had resurfaced and she felt the way she had all those years ago. Would Maybeth forgive her? Would her mother and father forgive her for keeping it all to herself? She had been daddy's girl. She remembered feeling scared that if the secret had got out back then, her dad would have been so disappointed in her. His little girl. Tears started to form, but Avril blinked them away. There would be tears today she was sure, later. Not now. She filled the kettle and flicked the switch. Nate would be there in a couple of hours to collect her and Sophie. She would have a cup of tea and then go and get ready to face the day to come.

Pittenweem   July 2021

CHAPTER FORTY

Maybeth had dozed on and off all night. She had spoken to her birth mother yesterday and was meeting her today. When she had left Julie and Ronnie's house, she had gone straight to the café to fill Debbie in. Davy had been there too. He had stayed very quiet but was definitely smiling a lot. Maybeth wondered if Avril and Davy would meet up too.

After spending some time with them, she had gone back to her rooms and called her parents. They had been happy for her. Excited even. They asked Maybeth to take photos and send them on. They asked if she would say thank you to Avril for giving her to them. Maybeth said that she would pass on the thanks. Now, she had time to think about what was happening. From a work situation to a simple curiosity she had found her birth parents and in such a short time. She had watched these programmes where researchers, experts, social workers, police and TV folk spent months, sometimes even years looking for people. Maybeth wondered about what today would bring. Yesterday, she had seen a few photographs of Avril. She could see the resemblance but felt that she had Davy's looks more. Her build was Avril's, her eyes were a mix of Ronnie and Davy. She had enjoyed looking through the albums of Nate and Sophie. Her half-brother and half-sister. She smiled at the thought of having siblings. She hoped that they would want to meet her someday. She went to the bathroom and switched on the shower. She would get ready and go for breakfast. Debbie was good at settling nerves. She had a couple of hours before she would be getting picked up by her grandfather. She told him she could bring her car or walk up the hill, the day was going to be nice, but, Ronnie had insisted that he come for her. She tested the running spray and stepped into the water, getting ready for the day ahead.

Pittenweem   July 2021

CHAPTER FORTY – ONE

The journey to the coast was pleasant. Nate and Jess bantered back and forth in the front and Avril looked out the window in the back beside Sophie who was fiddling around with her phone.

As the names of the towns and villages became more familiar to Avril she could feel her stomach start to lurch. There was where the little sweet shop used to be, now a Thai Restaurant. Over there was where Avril, Davy and Davina would cycle. Down lanes which led out into the country and here were the fields where they would hide in the muddy tractor ruts for hours at a time during long summer holidays. Round this bend that they were approaching Avril knew that you would see the sea rising up over the brow of the hill. Avril used to freewheel her bike down this hill, legs out, hands on the handles, finger hovering over the brake just in case she met with a car coming up the hill with the wind fanning her hair out behind her.

Unconsciously, she opened the window to smell the salty air. She pulled her mask down and there it was . She closed her eyes and took in a lungful of the familiar air. As she exhaled and opened her eyes she felt Sophie watching her. She fixed her mask back over her nose and returned Sophies gaze. Sophie had a smile playing on her lips.

' Nearly home mum,' Sophie said gently.

'Nearly.' Avril replied smiling and reaching for her hand.

Soon they were parking in Julie and Ronnie's driveway. Nate turned and looked at his mum.

'OK mum, this is it, we'll go down to the harbour for an hour you go in and meet Maybeth.'

Avril felt terror clouding over her. Sophie hugged her.

'It's all going to be fine. She's one of us. How could it be anything else.'

Jess joined in.

"You've got this, Avril.'

Avril sighed and undid her seatbelt.

'Thanks ' she managed as she got out of the car.

Nate gave a toot as he drove off and Avril walked to the front door. She had never been in this house. It was new and strange. Should she ring the doorbell? Before she could decide the front door opened and her mother ran out and silently took her in her arms where they both dissolved into tears. This was the second time today Avril had teared up and she knew there were lots more tears still to come.

Pittenweem   July 2021

CHAPTER FORTY-TWO

Ronnie's car crunched onto the gravel driveway. By this time Julie and Avril had gone inside. They had stood crying in each other's arms and apologizing for a time. Avril was sorry that she had kept it all from her mum and Julie apologized for being too busy to notice at the time. They hugged until Julie had ushered her daughter inside to wash her face in readiness to meet Maybeth.

In the car Maybeth and Ronnie had chatted to start with, but by the time they approached the house the air was quiet and filled with a nervous energy. Ronnie pulled up and stopped the car. As the engine ceased he looked at his granddaughter and smiled.

'Are you OK?'

'I'm good thanks,' Maybeth replied undoing her seatbelt and opening the door quickly.

'Let's go' she said as she jumped out of the car.

Ronnie continued undoing his seatbelt. She had looked terrified under that mask. This was a huge moment for her. For them all. He knew Avril would be feeling the same.

As she opened the front door Maybeth could hear voices. Soft voices and then they stopped. Maybeth stood still. She needed a moment. Ronnie came in and put his hand gently on her shoulder. Taking a quick breath, Maybeth entered the room and there she was. Her birth mother. Avril stood taking in this young woman who looked so confident. She was beautiful.

Her hair was long and dark. She wasn't tall but the ease with which she had walked into the room had made her seem taller. The shape of her eyes was Davy but the colour was her dad's. Avril could tell that Maybeth was smiling under the mask as her eyes were crinkled at the corners.

'Hi' Maybeth said gently as she took a seat. ' under normal circumstances I would be hugging you.' she said letting in a short laugh.

Avril immediately felt at ease and sat down in the armchair opposite. , She laughed too. In her head she had been going to meet a younger, shy, angry version of a daughter, but this young woman was self-assured, easy in her own skin. The people who had parented her had done a good job if first impressions could be gone by.

'I'm so glad you found us.' Avril said. Just then, Julie entered with a tea tray set for two.

'Your dad and I will be out in the garden if you need us.'

The day was nice so being in the garden would not be a chore for Ronnie, and Julie would potter about too to try and take her mind off what was happening in here. She put the tray on the coffee table and left the room.

'Shall I play mum?' Maybeth said.

Avril heard the word and immediately caught her breath. Again, Maybeth had called her 'mum' on the phone last night and she had been happy. Now all she felt was guilt. How could she be mum? She didn't deserve the title. She could feel Maybeth looking at her.

'Are you alright?' Maybeth asked with concern in her voice. She noticed Avril had gone pale and knew the word had hit a nerve.

'It's a lot, isn't it?' Maybeth said.

Avril nodded.

'How do you take your tea?' Maybeth asked.

'Just a little milk please.' Avril responded.

When the tea was poured and they were both sitting comfortably distanced with their masks off, Avril spoke.

'I'm so sorry for not keeping you,' she looked straight at Maybeth.

'I have always loved you and not a day has gone by where I haven't thought about you. I need to know that you've had a good life.'

Tears were suddenly overwhelming her.

'I had a great life' Maybeth responded happily. ' my parents were amazing. I went to a good school, I had lots of nice friends, I went to University and got a business degree, I have a great job in an estate agency and a nice flat in a good part of London. Life is good.'

She took a sip of her tea and continued.

' I must admit, I was told I was adopted when I was eight, but I never ever felt different and had no desire to find you.' She paused.

'I'm sorry if that seems cruel, but it's the truth. I wasn't even curious about you until I came to work here two weeks ago.'

'How did you find us?' Avril asked.

Maybeth chuckled.

'It's a very small place. It said on my birth certificate where I was born and when a house was given to the estate agency I was asked to come and sell it, which I did, and as you will know, small towns and foreign accents lead to nosy folk and thousands of questions.'

Maybeth took a breath and laughed. Avril laughed too.

'Which is exactly why I left. Tell me more.'

She was beginning to relax now. Maybeth's way of explaining things reminded Avril so much of Sophie.

'I use the café on the harbour to eat in most evenings and have become quite friendly with Debbie, the owner. Avril's brow furrowed trying to recall a Debbie, and failing.

'One day, in fact, five days ago.' Maybeth chuckled. Had it really only been five days? 'I was in my car and a man recognized me. It was my dad.'

Avril took a sharp intake of breath. Davy was still here. Maybeth watched Avril's reaction.

'I've been getting to know him. He's a lovely man.'

There was silence.

Maybeth could feel the pain from her mother. She really wanted to go to her and hug the pain away. To tell her that everything would be alright. She looked at her now. Taking in the hair, although starting to grey, the same colour as her own. Her eyes were darker than Maybeth's, but she could see that they were happy eyes. At present they were blurred with tears. Her mouth had the same shape as Maybeth's too.

Eventually Avril spoke.

'I've not seen him since we were seventeen.'

Maybeth finished her tea, which had started to go cold and placed her cup on the tray.

' He's told me his side. He is very remorseful. He carried a lot of guilt and pain too,' Maybeth could see Avril wince ' but that's in the past. Let's talk about my brother and sister.'

Avril shook her head and smiled. This girl was really like Sophie, able to bring things round and ease the tension. They spent an hour talking about Nate and Sophie before Julie popped her head round the door.

'I hear laughing and a lot of it. Can we come in now? It's starting to cool off out there.' She shivered for effect which made Avril and Maybeth laugh some more. Avril felt like a schoolgirl again. This moment had released something inside her and she felt lighter than she ever had.

Ronnie and Julie came in and joined the chat from the sofa.

Maybeth had said she wanted to stay in touch, to call her mum if that was OK, to meet her siblings. She had also told Avril that her parents said 'Thank you' and they were so grateful to her for gifting them a longed-for child. This had turned Avril into a sobbing heap, but Maybeth had chatted easily and let Avril cry.

'Are you ready to call Nate and Sophie and tell them to come up?' Ronnie asked, holding up his phone 'Sophie's texted twelve times already.'

'I would love to meet them. ' Maybeth said excitedly.

'Why don't we meet them down at the harbour?' Avril suggested 'Then I'll show you all where Maybeth was born.'

'Yes,' nodded Maybeth quietly 'yes, please.'

Pittenweem   July 2021

CHAPTER FORTY-THREE

Debbie had noticed the three visitors as they entered the café. They had ordered lattes and scones. She was sure she recognized the younger girl but couldn't think where from. They were not local, she knew that. As soon as they had taken their masks off to eat, she had recognized the younger woman. As she busied herself making the drinks for another lot of customers, she saw Davy enter and take a seat at the window. The smaller tables were seated at the windows. They could take two people and due to the government restrictions, the larger ones could take four at the maximum. Debbie hoped she would be able to stay open. She had closed up the last time there had been a Covid lockdown and had furloughed her staff. She knew that next month she would have to pay the 10% towards the furlough scheme and didn't know if she would be able to. It was a dark time and the only time she had thought about selling up. Maybe Maybeth handled commercial property sales too. Debbie shook the thought from her head. It would keep for another time. Today she had customers to attend to and keep her happy. She served the drinks she had been preparing and wandered over to Davy.

'Hi Davy. What will it be today?'

'A full Scottish and a cup of tea please Debbie.' Davy seemed more cheerful than usual.

'Someone's in a good mood' Debbie smiled 'care to share?'

'Och, its nothing special. I just had a good talking to myself and I'm going to spend some time off the boat for a while. Maybe see a bit of the world.'

Debbie grinned.

'That girl of yours is having an effect on you.'

'All for the good,' Davy grinned back ' all for the good.'

Then the smile slipped and he froze.

'What is it?' Debbie asked registering the change in Davy's posture.

Davy nodded towards the table of three.

'That girl, its Maybeth but younger.' He whispered

Debbie threw her hands up in the air dramatically.

'That's who she reminded me of. I knew I recognized her.' Debbie smiled ' I wonder if they know she's here?

'I wonder if they brought their mother?' Davy said, his voice thick with emotion.

Pittenweem   July 2021

CHAPTER FORTY-FOUR

Maybeth stood at the sink in Julie and Ronnie's small downstairs bathroom looking at herself in the mirror. She had just met the woman who had given birth to her. She seemed nice, but Maybeth was feeling something she couldn't understand. Why had Avril not told her parents? They would have helped her, Maybeth was certain. At that moment she felt anger towards the woman in the room across the hallway. Now she was to meet her siblings. Half an hour ago she would have gone willingly but, she needed time. Things were moving too quickly. She was feeling overwhelmed. Overwhelmed was a feeling at odds to her normal. She didn't want to do this meet and greet. She wasn't ready at the moment. All she wanted to do was go back to the safety of her rooms and phone Laura for a long chat and some reassurance. She needed to recalibrate. Maybeth didn't usually cry easily, but now she could feel the tears starting to cloud her vision. She ran the cold tap and splashed water onto her face. Turning the tap off and drying her face with a fluffy peach hand towel she unlocked the bathroom door and headed back into the living room and her newly found family.

'Listen, ' she said as they all looked up at her. ' Do you mind if I meet the rest another day, I'm feeling a bit overwhelmed.' Maybeth continued.

'I'm sorry that you've made the effort to come, but I'm feeling a little raw.'

Avril stood, ' of course.' She said.

'I'm not ready for anymore today,' Maybeth said ' I have questions. Questions that I didn't know I needed answers to.' She finished looking at Avril pointedly.

Avril took a step backwards. She had thought things were going well but this change had been what she had feared all her life. She nodded and sat back down,

' I'll give you my number and you can call me when you are ready.' Avril said gently. Maybeth took out her phone and Avril and Julie both put their numbers into it. Maybeth had remained standing.

'I'm sorry that I can't see the others today, but I think I just need to be by myself now. It's been lovely to meet you all and I will be in touch, but, I need to go. Goodbye.' Maybeth grabbed her jacket and handbag and left the house.

Julie looked at Ronnie and Avril. Ronnie had been about to offer Maybeth a lift but this had happened very suddenly. Avril let out the breath she had been holding and shook her head.

'I thought we were all getting on well' Julie said.

'Mum,' said Avril ' I was expecting it. Its a lot for her to process. I think she's angry with me.'

Ronnie nodded. ' She'll go through all sorts of feelings.'

'We better let the kids know she's not coming' Julie said.

'I'll call them now and get them to come up.' Avril said picking up her phone and dialing Nate's number. Julie began to clear away the tea things. A horrible feeling was creeping over her that Maybeth wouldn't call. A feeling that said that Maybeth would decide that she didn't want to know them and she would just get on with her life. Avril was sharing this feeling, but it was what she felt she deserved. She had abandoned this baby and now her baby would abandon her. Karma was something she believed in and now it was out to get her. She finished the call with Nate and then helped her mum load the dishwasher. She had achieved something today. She had managed a visit back to her birth town and felt okay being here. She could come back and explore again. She really hoped she would see Maybeth again soon. She was ready to answer anything. The look she had seen in Maybeth's eyes had been of hurt, anger and fear. She was acquainted with them all and all she wanted to do now was remove them from her daughter.

Pittenweem   July 2021

CHAPTER FORTY-FIVE

Maybeth closed the blind, took off her shoes and jacket and flopped on to the bed on her stomach. What had happened at Julie and Ronnie's house? These feelings had been so alien, to her.

Unnatural. She had enjoyed meeting Avril. She had been talking freely and then…what?

The thought of meeting her children. People who had the same mother, the same blood who had been allowed to live with Avril in their lives/ Maybeth felt bad for thinking this. She had had a great upbringing. She lifted her phone and called Laura.

'Hello stranger,' Laura chirped as she answered.

'Hi,' Maybeth blurted ' I met my birth mother today.

'Wow! How did that go?' Laura answered.

Maybeth told her the whole story. It tumbled from her like water over pebbles and when she was finished Laura spoke.

'The feelings you're having I would think are normal under the circumstances,' she said.

'But I met my birth father and its all jokey and nice.' Maybeth groaned.

'He doesn't have kids, does he?' Laura asked.

'No,' Maybeth replied 'Just me.'

'It's a jealousy thing, these other kids had what you didn't and you're feeling resentful. Its not fair.'

'You're right. It's not fair.' Maybeth shot back.

'But what is not fairer,' Laura continued " is that they never got to meet me and you did.' She started to giggle.

Maybeth smiled. Laura always knew how to make her feel better.

"How's work?' Maybeth asked.

'No,' said Laura ' we are not talking about work. You'll want to come back and you need this time away.' Laura said with finality.

'OK, ' Maybeth said. "I'm coming back next week no matter what happens.'

'Then go and do what you have to do, and I'll see you next week. Keep me up to date.' Laura said and hung up.

Maybeth clung to the phone. Do what she had to do? She had to talk to Debbie and her dad.

Pittenweem   July 2021

CHAPTER FORTY-SIX

'What if she never wants to meet us?' Sophie moaned. They were sitting around Julie's dining room table.

' I don't want to go if there's a chance she'll change her mind' said Nate 'I think we should head back to the café. The menu looked amazing for evening meals.'

'I don't want to do anything that'll startle her, ' Avril said, ' This is huge for us all, but I also want to take a walk along the harbour while I'm here.'

Nate smiled ' How does that sound Jess?' Jess had been quiet up until now.

'I'm a bit tired. Would you mind if I stayed here with your gran?' Jess asked. Julie nodded ' I can make you a wee sandwich' Julie said, Jess nodded in return.

'Right, who wants a walk?' Nate said standing up and stretching his long arms. Sophie grabbed her jacket and Avril stood too.

'I'll follow you down in the car,' Ronnie said ' that way I can bring you back up when you've eaten.

Avril chose not to take the church pathway but chose a less emotional route for them all. As she walked, she recognized the pebble dashed walls of Mr and Mrs McGlone's house, always so neat and tidy with colourful potted plants outside the front door. The route was a descent down to the harbour and she could already smell the harbour smells and hear the gulls as the day started to turn into evening. It was just after six o'clock and it was still light.

They cut through the small lanes that wound down and walked through the archway which led onto the harbour-side. Soon they were standing looking onto the water. Avril scanned the boats and there she was *The Betty Smith*. Without a thought she walked towards where it stood on the pebbled shore and put out her hand to touch the rough paintwork. Davy had worked on this boat when it was new. He had spoken to her with excitement in his voice about having the chance to break in a new boat. The memories of Davy came flooding back to her. Was he living nearby? Could he see her now? The bench was still here too. The bench that she had sat upon when she knew she had a decision to make. Always this bench. The urge to sit on it now was so strong.

She walked over and ran her hand over the back edge. 'Hello old friend' she said as she sat down. Sophie was standing at the railings talking to Nate about the colour of the buoys. She chattered on as Nate patiently listened to her, indulging his sister's enthusiasm. Avril was so proud of her children and so grateful that they had come. Maybe the thoughts Maybeth was having were about her siblings. Avril hoped that she would have the chance to get to know Maybeth properly. She had loved the chat that they had had together. She had spent the whole time drinking in every word Maybeth had spoken. Her accent, her laugh, her inflections. All remembered and stored away safely.

'I wonder what gran's house looks like now that it's guest rooms?' Sophie said as Nate and she walked over to their mother. They all looked behind them to where The Old Chandlery Guest Rooms stood. Avril liked the new name. Sophie started to walk towards it.

'Where are you going, Soph?' Avril called out to her.

'I'm just going to take a peek in the window.' Sophie answered with a giggle. She rushed over and stood at the window just as the blind shot up and she stood face to face with her sister.

Pittenweem   July 2021

CHAPTER FORTY-SEVEN

Maybeth opened the blind and let out a scream. There was a face staring in the window at her. The face looked as if it had let out a scream too. Within seconds it was joined by two other faces. One of which she had only just been thinking about. She took one of the hands, which had both been at her mouth with the shock and pointed it at Avril. Avril pointed back and then raised her hands, palm forward in a gesture of apology. Maybeth raised a finger. ' stay there' she said. She grabbed her key and rushed outside onto the doorstep. Sophie and Nate had not realised who she was and Sophie was beside herself with embarrassment. 'I'm so sorry,' she said as Maybeth appeared. ' I was just looking because my gran used to live here and we spent happy days here and I didn't mean to scare you.' She stopped talking. ' You're Maybeth?' she asked in utter amazement.

Maybeth looked at Avril and then Sophie with a wry smile. For all that she hadn't wanted to meet them, this was quite amusing. It was probably the perfect way to break the ice and something that could be laughed about in years to come.

'and you must be Sophie?' she replied, biting her lip to stop a giggle from escaping. Poor Sophie's face was as red as the lobster Debbie was forever putting on her dish of the day board.

'I didn't know she would do that' Avril said adding a plea. ' Forgive us?'

'It's fine, Maybeth replied. ' Look, I'm just going for something to eat in the café. Why don't you all join me, and we can chat there?'

'If, you're sure?' Nate asked.

'I'm sure.' Maybeth answered looking at Nate. He was taller than her and quite handsome. He didn't look as much like Avril as Sophie and she did but she could tell they were related.

'Let me grab my bag and I'll be right with you.' Maybeth said as she turned and ran into the rooms.

Sophie turned to Avril and looped her arm through hers. 'Mum' she whispered, 'I'm so sorry.'

'It's fine.' Avril said echoing Maybeth's sentiment and she started to believe that it might well be.

Pittenweem   July 2021

CHAPTER FORTY-EIGHT

Debbie had put the last of the days dishes away and finding it quiet, was taking the time to chat to the chef about tomorrow's specials and menu for the next week, when the door opened for the first of the evening's diners. It was some of the people from earlier and an older man and middle aged woman, with Maybeth bringing up the rear.

'Good evening.' Debbie trilled, excitement radiating from her. This was Maybeth's family. Davy had gone home shortly after the trio had left. Debbie was quite glad that Davy wasn't here. She didn't know if he would have been able to cope with so much emotion in the one day. This was probably the most excitement he had ever had, she thought. Debbie had grown up here, but was quite up to date with city fashions and trends, but Davy was a dyed-in-the-wool born and bred little harbour villager. He was more at home on the water if truth be told. On land, he was lost.

'Evening' they answered.

Debbie ushered them over to two tables at the back which were a little more private. The ruling was tables of four and they were a five, so they would have to separate themselves. This area was perfect for a new family to chat. She used it for intimate dinners, proposals, marriage guidance sessions and all sorts of life planning and affirming moments.

She was sure Maybeth would appreciate the gesture. The café would be filling up soon. She had a couple of large bookings and the evening was nice which meant visitors descending for a walk along the harbour front and the chance of a meal in the cafe. The lido was a nice walk for after a meal too. It was gentle and the lapping sounds of the water could be relaxing and pleasant too.

Maybeth sat down with her mother on one side and Sophie on the other. Nate sat at the next table with Ronnie who had parked outside and met them at the door. Sophie continued to stare at Maybeth as she looked at the menu. Maybeth felt her eyes burning into her and looked up.

'Are you alright?' she asked Sophie.

'I'm so sorry,' Sophie breathed ' I just can't stop looking at you, I'm scared it's a dream. I've wanted to meet you since I was seven.'

Maybeth gasped ' Seven ? Really ? That long?'

Sophie nodded. 'I've named dolls after you, she chuckled.

Maybeth smiled and slowly shook her head. This was her little sister and at that moment she felt loved. This girl had known about Maybeth, she really hadn't been hidden. She turned her face to Avril.

'So, why did you never come back here?'

The question had been playing on her mind. The sharp tone had surprised her as the words left her mouth, but the question needed to be asked. Avril put down her menu, her stomach heaving, She looked at Sophie and then at Nate before answering.

'It was too painful. I didn't want Davy to see me. I didn't want any reminders of what I'd given up.' Tears started to form. ' I went back to the manse to get you, but you were gone. I always loved you.'

Maybeth smiled.

' But your parents?'

'I wanted to tell them. I was surprised the kids never told them.' Avril looked at Nate and Sophie.

'I think because you weren't with us, we only spoke about you with mum.' Nate said. ' She seemed so sad when she spoke about you and we associated being with gran and grandad as a happy time. Is that bad?'

Ronnie covered Nate's hand with his own and Maybeth shook her head.

'No, its not bad. It's honest and it makes sense, Thank you Nate.'

It was the first time she had spoken his name. As she looked at him she imagined the little boy he must have been and she desperately wanted to hug him. What was with her? She was getting mushy. Maybeth didn't do sentiment. She picked up the menu.

'Right, what's everyone having?'

Pittenweem   July 2021

CHAPTER FORTY-NINE

Jess loved coming to Julie and Ronnie's house. Julie was like another granny to her. She always made her feel comfortable, but today, there was no comfortable. She was feeling sick. Sick, tired and her stomach was cramping. Nate had been away for an hour and a half. She had managed to eat half of a cream cheese and cucumber sandwich and a cup of tea, but she now felt sick and dizzy, Julie noticed.

'Jess, I don't like the colour of you.'

At these words Jess flopped over onto her side. Julie rushed to her to check. Jess was unconscious but breathing steadily.

Julie put her into the recovery position, grabbed the phone and called for an ambulance and then she called Nate. Julie then sat with Jess and waited for help to arrive. Not long after, the door burst open and Nate, Sophie and Avril rushed in. Nate immediately going to his wife's side. He looked pale and worried. Julie stepped back to give them room.

'Where's the ambulance? Is she going to be alright? What's wrong with her?' Sophie garbled. Firing questions rapidly around the room. Ronnie and Maybeth entered followed by the paramedics. They had arrived as they were getting out of the car. The main hospital was 10 miles away in St Andrew's, but fortunately there had been an ambulance dropping off at the cottage hospital along the road and they had been able to reach it before it returned. The paramedics busied themselves checking Jess's stats, as the group gathered round. Julie took Sophie into her arms. Maybeth, Avril and Ronnie stood watching, tight lipped, anxious and grim faced. The paramedics got Jess, carefully onto a trolley and wheeled her out and into the ambulance with an oxygen mask fitted in place. Nate had been answering question after question. No, she hadn't been taking drugs or alcohol. No, she didn't take seizures or have epilepsy. Yes, she was taking prescribed medication. Yes, there was a possibility that she could be pregnant. Yes, she led a healthy lifestyle. Yes, she was able to have a blood transfusion and yes, she was an organ and blood donor. The questions were worrying but needed to be asked. Nate and Avril got into Nate's car and followed the blue lights all the way. The decision had been taken that Maybeth would stay with Sophie and Julie and Ronnie's house. Time ticked by. Jess was rushed immediately to the operating theatre. They had been told at the hospital that no-one could get in due to the strict Covid rules, so Nate and Avril were sitting quietly in the car, each lost in their own thoughts. Twice, Nate got out of the car to stretch his legs and pace. Avril felt helpless watching her son worry. She remembered a time when Chris had looked like that too. Nate shared so many of his father's mannerisms and his looks. They were interrupted by the sound of Nate's phone ringing. It had been three hours Avril counted as she checked the time on her phone. She heard the faint voice of a man as she strained to listen in on the conversation.

'Yes, but is she going to be Ok?" Nate was asking. He had his eyes closed as if he was praying for a positive answer. Then he sighed.

'Thank you, Dr.' He looked over at his mum and nodded. 'Okay, so what exactly does it mean going forward?' he asked with more certainty in his voice. Nate was good at switching between personal and professional dialogue. Now he had gone into business, no nonsense, taking charge mode. This was serious and he needed to know everything he had to know in order to help his wife. He had been through this before with the crash but now she had gone through an ectopic pregnancy. The doctor had just explained that the baby had been growing in the tube just outside the womb. Jess had been about six weeks pregnant so they had caught it early enough that no real damage had been done and Jess should be able to conceive and carry to term in the future. She would have to stay in hospital for a few days and could Nate get some clothes and toiletries for her. The doctor had also added that Jess had requested a packet of custard creams. Nate laughed. Jess loved a custard cream. He thanked the doctor and hung up. He then relayed everything to Avril. Avril sighed and smiled sadly to Nate. Poor Jess. She took Nate's hand and squeezed it gently. Nate squeezed back, let go and quietly started the engine.

Pittenweem   July 2021

CHAPTER FIFTY

Debbie had watched the way in which Maybeth was interacting with the others. It was obvious to her that she belonged with these people. She looked like them and, although Maybeth had seemed quite nervous when they sat down, she had quickly relaxed and was now holding her own in the conversation and almost taken control. Debbie liked Maybeth. She was no-nonsense and Debbie could see why her company had sent her to sell the house. She was a people person, very charismatic. She sold that house quickly and with no problems. Debbie felt a small pang of sadness. Maybeth would be leaving to go back to her life in London. Avril had paid the bill once they had eaten. Maybeth had said she would pay, but Avril was stubborn and wouldn't hear of it. Debbie could see where Maybeth got her determination from too. It was hard to tell under masks if people were smiling or not these days, but Debbie could hear it in their voices as they left the café that they were all happy and well-fed customers. She could hear them laughing and finishing each other's sentences. She could see where Davy would fit in here too. Even though he was quite a quiet man, he would be the silent backbone if it was allowed. Debbie wondered if Avril would ever meet with him.

She realized that she had been standing still, leaning over the counter. She had been polishing cutlery and closing up. It was a quieter night so she had decided to close earlier and sent the chef and the 2 waiting staff home. She loved this café but tonight she was tired. She finished off the polishing and cleaned out the coffee machines. Cold coffee smelled a lot different from hot coffee she thought as she tipped it into the binbag. She hated the feel of the cold wet filter. The heaviness like a loaded nappy. She felt the usual bile rise in her throat as she tied the top of the binbag in a knot. She jumped suddenly as she heard a loud bang and then shouting and screaming. From where she stood she could see some people running to the right of her shop. She ran to the door and opened it.

'Quick!' someone shouted.

'He's not breathing,' another voice was saying 'someone call an ambulance.'

'I will.' Debbie answered, retreating back into the shop and grabbing the phone. She quickly called the ambulance and gave the call handler as much information as she could, which was barely any as she had not seen what had happened and didn't know who had been injured. She ran back outside and let the people attending the person that the ambulance was on its way. As she looked now, she could see a man lying at a very peculiar angle. His body twisted one way, his legs another. He had been hit by a motorbike. The young biker was sitting up, dazed on the pavement. This looked bad, Debbie thought. There were a few people gathered now attending to the man, but the biker sat alone. She saw a police car coming towards the scene so she went back inside the café. There were enough people out there. She hoped the man, whoever he was, was going to be alright. She would have to wait here now as her car was parked just where the scene was playing out outside and she didn't have the energy to climb the steep hill and walk the distance to her flat. She took a can of orange from the fridge and sat down at a table. She had locked the door and put the main lights out so as not to attract any customers. She took out her phone and went to the games app. She didn't know how long she would have to wait and needed something mind numbing to block out what was happening outside.

Pittenweem   July 2021

CHAPTER FIFTY-ONE

Sophie had not stopped talking for the whole time they had waited for news. Maybeth noticed that she was agitated and judging by the way Sophie kept nibbling her nails when Maybeth was answering all the questions that Sophie was firing at her, she guessed that this girl lived on her nerves. Maybeth felt as if she was on a speed dating session but one where she didn't have to move from table to table and there was no hot date at the end of it. Sophie really had wanted to know everything about her right down to how many, if any tattoo's she had. She had one. A small bumblebee. She had been quite active in the Save The Bees campaign a few years ago and her and Laura had been persuaded by another friend, Jax to have a tattoo done. She didn't regret it. It could be a lot worse. She had once had a client who had his two sons baby pictures on her calves and the eyes were like cartoon eyes. He had been wearing shorts to his appointment with her and as he was walking in front of her, she hadn't been able to take her eyes off them. She had at one point had to excuse herself from the room so that he didn't see her giggling.

Sophie's questions had stopped on Avril's phone call. When they were given the news that Jess would be OK. She had gone quiet. Maybeth used the silence to leave the room. Julie and Ronnie were there to comfort Sophie if she needed it. Maybeth went into garden and sat on the bench. She wasn't used to so much family activity. She had never had to consider so many feelings and emotion and right now she was feeling a little bit guilty as she didn't know how to handle this. This strong, independent, business minded woman was at a loss as to what to do. She scrolled through her phone and found a number that Debbie had given her for the café. She would call Debbie. They hadn't long left the café and had just been getting into the car when Julie had called, so Debbie was unaware of anything that had happened. Maybeth had introduced them all to Debbie during the ordering of the meal and they had all exchanged some friendly chat. She dialed Debbie's number. It was engaged. She would try again later. Above Debbie's name in her phone numbers, she had saved Davy (Dad). She pressed on it and saw the green call sign. She let it ring for what seemed like an age before hanging up. She had a fleeting feeling of despair but shook it off before it became effective. Poor Jess. She had lost her baby. It was odd. One lost, one found. She hoped that Jess would be able to have another. The doctor had said she could. Maybeth stood up and walked back into the house. That couple of minutes had been ample sufficient to recharge her batteries for whatever was to come.

Pittenweem   July 2021

CHAPTER FIFTY-TWO

Debbie watched from the café window as the ambulance moved slowly away. She knew that was never a good sign. If an ambulance wasn't blue lighting, there was a very high chance that the man hadn't made it. She hoped it hadn't been anyone she knew. It was bad enough someone may have lost their life, but she didn't like bad news. The thought was sending tears to her eyes. The police had taken the biker in the police car and the bike had been carefully loaded onto a police recovery vehicle. There were still a couple of officers going over the ground for loose particles of bike. The people who had gathered had moved over towards the harbour in a huddle. With the size of this place being so small, everyone would know what had happened in an hour. That was one thing Debbie both admired and disliked about this village. The gossip could be horrendous, but the people always rallied round when there was things needed to be done. She should probably make a move for home. She grabbed her jacket and switched off the lights. It was starting to get dark. So much for her early night. She sighed as she stepped outside and locked the door.

Mark Vaughan had locked up the office and was striding down the street, happily when the bike hit him. His last thoughts had been of how he would spend the large commission he would get for selling the old harbourmaster's house. The bike hadn't been going too fast but a cat had shot out from an alleyway towards the gulls and the biker had swerved sharply to avoid it and merely clipped him according to eye witnesses. Mark had fallen and banged his head on the cobbled ground. He had died instantly.

Debbie crossed the street to where the small crowd were still talking. She recognized them all. Jessie Stipe who ran the ice cream parlour, Annie something who was a childminder, Lorna and Peter Cunningham the lawyers and old Charlie who was a frequent customer of Debbie's.

Mark had been into the café on occasion too. This was such a horrible and tragic accident. The police had been satisfied that that was what it was, so they hadn't needed to cordon off or close down the area. There had been some witnesses too. There was still some of Mark's blood on the cobbles where he had fallen, and Lorna was pouring bottled water on it to flush it away. With the Scottish weather being as changeable as it was, it wouldn't take long to wash away in a heavy shower. There would have to be a postmortem of course, due to Mark's age, even though there were no suspicions, and someone would have to replace him in the business. This was all being relayed by the Annie somebody. Debbie frowned. The man had just lost his life and here they were replacing him. It made her think of her own mortality. These things always did. She said her goodbyes and made her way towards her car. The group had obviously been looking for a catalyst as Debbie saw them disperse and make their way home too. Debbie clicked on her seatbelt, started the engine and finally made her way home for the night.

Pittenweem   July 2021

CHAPTER FIFTY-THREE

Maybeth woke up worried the next morning. After last nights events she had slept badly. Ronnie had taken Sophie to meet Avril and Nate at the hospital and they had all gone home from there. Maybeth had gone home and had a shower and a glass of wine before going to bed. Avril had called just as she was falling asleep to apologise and to ask if she could come back and meet up in a couple of days. Maybeth had agreed that that would be fine. She was glad that she had met her but she was now also glad that she had some time to clear her head before the next meet up. Maybeth had called her parents and told them everything. They had been happy for her, concerned for Jess and laughed when she told them about her chatty, bubbly sister.

'She sounds like fun.' Mum had said.

Next, Maybeth called her friend Nuala. She just needed to speak to someone that she knew well. Nuala was that someone. They had been friends since Year 1. Nuala was now a biologist and was often abroad, usually in the Nordic countries, doing biologist things. She had tried to explain what she did to Maybeth on a number of occasions, but Maybeth still didn't really know. Something to do with tectonic plate drilling.

Nuala was, as always, excited to hear Maybeth's news. She was currently in an Ice Bar in Sweden with and Australian scientist colleague called Nigel. He had the loudest laugh Nuala had ever heard and she had been trying unsuccessfully, for the past hour, to ditch him. Nuala had told him when her phone rang that it was her lesbian lover to try and put him off, but his eyes had widened, and he'd boomed stridently

'I love a challenge.'

Maybeth had laughed as she imagined Nuala rolling her eyes. She had needed this call. This morning she was going to see Davy. Not being able to contact him last night had made her feel uneasy. As she was getting her shoes on there was a knock at the door. She opened it to see, Liz the new owner of The Chandlery. She had just popped by to see if there was anything she needed. Maybeth thanked her and said that everything was fine.

'Terrible shame about that man.' Liz commented.

Maybeth hadn't been looking for a long conversation, but, obviously Liz was in no hurry and had something to impart.

'What's that?' Maybeth asked.

'The man that died outside yesterday,' Liz answered ' he got hit by a bike and fell and banged his head. Died immediately, God rest his soul.'

'Outside of here?' Maybeth asked with the shock apparent in her voice.

'Aye, in front of Debbie's café. Quite a young man too. Worked in the estate agents. In fact, you might have known him.'

'Mark?' asked Maybeth.

'Aye, that was his name.'

Maybeth froze.

'Are you OK, love?'

Liz ushered Maybeth inside away from the door and on to the bed.

'Sit here and I'll get you a glass of water.'

Maybeth shook her head trying to stop the news from filtering in. She had only recently met Mark and he had seemed like a nice guy. Poor Mark, he had had years left and one moment had taken them away. Maybeth stood up.

'I'm sorry Liz, can I leave the water? I think I need to take a walk.'

Liz, who had been running the cold tap, turned it off again.

'Of course, I'll walk you out.'

They left the building. Liz walking towards the next house where she owned property too and Maybeth towards Davy's house. She stopped at the railings beside the *Betty Smith* and took some deep breaths. The airs saltiness mingling with the smell of the rain. She continued her short journey and soon was standing at Davy's front door. It was ajar.

'Davy!' she said as she knocked. There was no reply, so she let herself in not knowing what she would find.

Edinburgh   July 2021

CHAPTER FIFTY-FOUR

Avril had had a restless night too. She had tossed and turned throughout. Nate had managed to speak to Jess on the phone. She was Ok but a bit sore after the miscarriage. Sophie had been tearful and quiet and had disappeared to her friend's house for a while. Avril was alone this morning. Her thoughts were on her eldest daughter. Her beautiful girl. Maybeth had a look of Ronnie, but the girl was Davy through and through. They had spoken a lot yesterday. Avril had worried that the conversation would dry up and that Maybeth would be angry with her. She worried that there would be bitterness and resentment, but Maybeth had had a good upbringing. She would certainly have had to leave home to go to University and London had much more opportunity on the doorstep than a little fishing village in the East coast of Scotland. Maybeth had been reluctant to meet Nate and Sophie which was perfectly understandable. These children had been with her. She had kept them. Avril felt a lurch in her stomach. The one she associated with guilt. She had been forgiven by Maybeth, but could she forgive herself? She picked up the phone. Maybeth had taken a selfie of them when she w as putting her number in. Avril looked at it now. Mother and daughter. Her firstborn. She had loved her even then when she had told herself she mustn't. She remembered back to the loneliness, the quiet fear, the guilt and the pain. Tears sprang unbidden and trickled down her face. As they reached her nose, she brushed them away. These tears were different now. They were tears of relief too. What was once lost had been found. Her daughter was now tangible. She had hugged her. They had obeyed all of the

Covid rules but the urge to hug had been too strong and she had hugged Maybeth to her as they parted. Maybeth had asked to be kept updated about Jess. She had been interested but not over emotional. There was a strength there. A resilience. One that Avril had recognised that she had in herself. She got out of bed and headed for the shower. Today she would look after Nate and tomorrow she would go back to Maybeth.

Pittenweem   July 2021

CHAPTER FIFTY-FIVE

Maybeth shouted again as she entered.

'Davy!' She heard a soft groan coming from the room at the back. The kitchen she remembered. As she entered, she could see him bent over by the door leading to the bathroom. She rushed over in trepidation. Davy was wearing a vest and a pair of trousers with braces attached. She hadn't seen this attire since she was a little girl and her mum had taken her to visit her nanny and pappa in Exeter. This was a first time that the thought that nanny Ella and pappa Joe had loved her and known that she was adopted too had come into her mind. Davy was groaning.

'Oh, Maybeth. I'm so glad you're here.'

'What's wrong? Maybeth asked, taking off her jacket.

'I think my back has gone. I can't seem to move.'

Maybeth moved round to assess the situation and burst out laughing.

'What's funny?' he asked looking annoyed and frozen in position

'Well, the good news is that your back hasn't gone,' Maybeth replied through giggles ' but, you do have your back trouser loop stuck in the latch.'

She helped him to remove the offending latch and he started to laugh too. They both had to hold onto chairs and fat tears of mirth were falling from their eyes. When they eventually caught their breath Maybeth asked.

'How long were you stuck?'

'About twenty minutes. I had got up and had a sink wash. Bath nights tonight.'

Maybeth smiled. Davy really was traditional. He carried on.

'I came into the kitchen to get my new shaving brush as the old one was falling apart and then I remembered I'd already taken it into the bathroom. As I turned,' he grinned ' my back went.'

They both started to giggle again.

'I'm glad it was just your trousers.' Maybeth said.

'And I'm glad you turned up.' Davy replied and then stopped. Maybeth looked at him and saw that his eyes were clouding.

'I really am glad you're here, Maybeth.'

'Me too,' she responded 'now go and have your shave and I'll put the kettle on.'

Davy smiled and shuffled into the bathroom. Maybeth filled the kettle and flicked the switch. For a man on his own Davy kept the place neat and tidy. She sat down at the table and giggled again. Davy was in his early fifties. She had seen the young trendies wearing braces or as she had recalled earlier her pappa Joe, but a forty something fisherman in Fife. Davy was not an old man, but he certainly dressed like one. She wondered if he would allow her to take him shopping. The kettle pinged and she set about making the cups of tea. She had remembered from the other night that Davy took a lot of sugar in his tea, so she left the milk and sugar out. He could add it himself when he came through. And there he was. Clean and smooth faced with a huge smile.

'That's better.' He beamed and he sat at the table beside Maybeth and added his milk and four spoonsful of sugar. Maybeth winced and felt her teeth scream. He wasn't looking at her so had missed the fleeting look of horror on her face.

'So,' she began ' the braces?'

Davy smiled at her. My belt broke and it's the only things I could find to keep my trousers up.' He smiled again. ' They were my dad's and possibly his dads before him. A family heirloom if you like. They'll be yours next.' His eyes were twinkling with mischief as he drained his teacup.

"I've an idea. Let's go shopping.' Maybeth suggested as if it had just come to her. ' We can trendy you up a bit.'

Davy looked at her in mock shock.

' And what would I want to be trendy for?'

'Well, you're not an old fossil, but your wardrobe could do with a revamp and...' she stopped.

'And?' Davy quizzed.

' And since you might be meeting my mother in the next few days .' She stopped again. Davy was shaking his head.

' She doesn't want to see me.' There was the pain back on his face.

'I think she might, and I also think she has to.'

Davy arose. Then sat back down. He had been going to argue but had no words. He put both elbows on the table and covered his face with his hands and then he started to sob.

'She broke my heart.' He cried.

Maybeth went to him and hugged him. She could care less for regulations today. This was her father, and he was upset.

'She knows what she did.' Maybeth whispered softly into his hair. Maybeth let him cry and when he was calm, they got ready and left the house. Davy's car was an older model Micra, but it was as clean and still had a new car smell. ' I don't use her much.' he said ' I usually get my shopping delivered and everything else I get from the wee shop here.'

'I love her.' Maybeth nodded in admiration.

As they drove to the nearest town Maybeth thought about the news Liz had told her about Mark Vaughn. She hadn't let herself think too much about it, but she now shared it with Davy. She would have to phone Laura. She was surprised that Laura hadn't called her, then she remembered that she had left her phone charging in the Old Chandlery. 'Oh well,' she thought, a day off-grid would be good for her. Davy and Maybeth went to the Old Town of St Andrew's and shopped, chatted, walked round the old cathedral grounds and the University, lunched on the Links and shopped some more. Davy bought three shirts, a pair of black jeans and two new belts. Maybeth treated him to a pair of good brown brogues and some comedy socks. When they got back Davy dropped Maybeth off at her rooms. As she got out of the car he said

'I've had the best day. Thank you.'

'Me too, dad' she answered.

Davy gasped. She had just called him dad. Maybeth gasped too. She hadn't meant to.

'No braces.' She chuckled.

"They'll be going into your heritage box the minute I get home' Davy chuckled back. They laughed as she shut the door and tapped the roof before giving him a wave. Maybeth was still smiling when she entered the room. She could hear her phone beeping and went over to unplug it. Five missed calls. That wasn't too bad. Four were from Laura and one was from Avril. She smiled when she saw her number. She had found her birth mother and father in the space of two weeks. Now they needed to re-find each other.

Edinburgh   July 2021

CHAPTER FIFTY-SIX

Avril had called Maybeth and left a message. She had thanked her once again for meeting up with her and asked her to let her know when she could come through again. She hoped it didn't come off as desperate. She would hate to frighten her away. She didn't want to annoy Maybeth and she was annoyed at herself for wanting this so much. She called Nate and he answered on the second ring.

'Hi mum, I was just about to ring you.'

Nate was one of life's optimists. Whatever was thrown at him he always seemed to remain upbeat.

'How's Jess?' Avril asked.

'She's ok. The doctor says that she can come home today. I'm just leaving to pick her up.'

Avril sighed. This was great news.

'Mum,' Nate continued ' it's really made me think about things. You know, about babies and being a dad and all that.'

Avril nodded her head 'Hmm" she muttered. She could see Nate bouncing a chubby, drooling baby on his knee and having the time of his life.

'I'm sure it'll happen when it happens.' He added quietly.

'I'm sure it will.' Avril agreed ' Jess just needs a bit of time to heal, emotionally as well as physically. It might feel raw to begin with. A loss is a loss, and she might cry a wee bit too. And so might you.'

'Whatever she needs mum, I'm there. Anyway, I better get on. I'll ask her to give you a call when she gets home.'

Avril said goodbye and hung up. She got ready to go to work. She had taken some time off but with the way the world was at the moment she had been asked to do an emergency cover. Two of her co-workers had tested positive for Covid 19, so she had said that she would go in. It would take her mind away from Maybeth for a little while until she was invited through to see her again. She put her jacket on and lifted her handbag and car key. She hoped that Maybeth would call soon. She started to hum a tune to drown out the thoughts and headed out to work.

Pittenweem   July 2021

CHAPTER FIFTY-SEVEN

'It's such a tragedy,' Laura was saying ' such a sad, tragic accident. We've shut down the branch for the week out of respect but we will need to find a replacement.' Maybeth heard the pause. She knew what was coming. The business part of her brain was always on high alert and when she heard it was Mark who had died she felt bad for going to the hard-wired '*what about the business*' section.

'Could you stay there until we find someone? Maybe set up the interviews?' Laura asked. 'It would mean more time with your family and help the company out of a massive hole.'

Maybeth was silent for a moment. She would ask Ronnie and Julie if she could stay with them as she had already told Liz at the Old Chandlery that she was intending to leave next week and it had quickly booked up for the summer months.

'Let me see what I can sort out. I'll get back to you later this afternoon.' She answered. Laura continued the chat, filling Maybeth in on all her news. Maybeth told her about the meet up with her mum, the shopping trip and braces fiasco with her dad and her trying to get her mother and father into the same room after twenty-nine years apart. Laura thought it was a fabulous idea.

'Record it.' She shrieked excitedly.

' I need, need, need to see the reaction. It could be a happily ever after or it could gloriously backfire and be the mother and father of all wars, no pun intended' she laughed.

Maybeth laughed too then grimaced. What had she got herself into.

'Anyway, I'll let you get on with playing Cupid and don't leave me hanging too long about the work thing.'

'I'll contact you as soon as I've spoken to the grandparents.'

They said their goodbyes and hung up. Maybeth looked down at her phone for a few seconds, trying to process it all. Again. Her life did seem to be full of surprises at the moment. Maybeth looked up Julie's number. She had saved it under Julie(Gran). It didn't take long for Julie to answer and when Maybeth told her what she needed, she could hear the excitement in the older woman's voice.

'Of course you can stay here. You can stay her for as long as you want.' The phone was then muffled as Julie held it away from her mouth to tell Ronnie the good news.

'Of course you can stay!' she heard Ronnie shouting from a distance in the background.

'Oh Maybeth sweetheart, its lovely. I'll just go and hoover and give it a wee dust and get your room ready for you.'

Maybeth had seen the room and was entirely sure there was no dust permitted to land at any time. Julie kept a spotless house and was a proud housekeeper. Her whole house was immaculate. Since Covid she had been even more meticulous than usual, buying all the sprays and disinfectants she could lay her hands on. Her bathrooms reeked of Forest Pine, but in a pleasant and reassuring way. Maybeth finished the call and hung up. She texted Laura and was rewarded with a thumbs up and two beaming smiley emojis. She needed a cup of tea. She put some music on her phone and busied herself making tea. Then she sat down and put her feet on the leather pouffe. She started to think about how she should begin Operation Reunite, then she texted Avril.

I'M FREE TOMORROW, 6PM IN THE CAFE?

Almost immediately she got a reply.

SEE YOU THERE X

Pitteweem   July 2021

CHAPTER FIFTY-EIGHT

She had called him dad. Davy had replayed the moment several times in his head. Maybeth had looked as taken aback as he had, but she hadn't looked worried about it. She had smiled and let the moment pass. She had called him dad. He would miss her when she left. He looked down at the jeans he had just put on with his new belt. A chuckle rose in his throat when he remembered how she had found him yesterday. He had made an arrangement to see Maybeth in Debbie's café this evening. He would wear his new clothes and shoes. Davy looked at himself in he mirror that hung over the fireplace. He could do with a haircut. Alan the Barber had a shop at the top of the hill.

He would take the car this morning and get a good cut. He called ahead, as the pandemic dictated that he could go in if no one else was in the shop. Davy said he had a slot in an hour. Davy put on the television and sat down to wait until it was time for his appointment. There was a programme on about men's style. He smiled as he thought back to his conversation with Maybeth at being trendy. What did he need to be trendy for? Who did he need to be trendy for? He flicked the channel as thoughts of Avril filled his head. This would be better, a programme about fixing up homes that were falling apart. He let himself imagine that he was fixing the houses up and what he would do to repair them. The time ticked and soon it was ten minutes to his appointment.

'Come on daddio,' he chuckled as he left the house, ' time to get trendy.'

Pittenweem   July 2021

CHAPTER FIFTY-NINE

Nate had collected Jess from the front of the hospital, where the porters had left her in a wheelchair. She was now safely home, on the couch eating her bodyweight in popcorn. She loved the mix of sweet and salty and on special occasions liked to buy herself a bag and eat it all in one sitting. Nate had bought this bag to cheer her up. Nate. What would she do without him ? The past forty-eight hours had been a blur. The normality of sharing lunch with Julie and then a sudden burst of excruciating pain in her abdomen followed by blackness as she fainted. She remembered drifting in and out, a blue light, medical people hidden behind masks talking to her as they crowded around her body.

She came too in the hospital. A kind doctor sitting by her bed when she awoke. He explained what had happened to her and what it would mean in the future. The processing of thought. There had been a baby and now there was none. She hadn't known how to feel. The foetus was only 6 weeks they said. Did this qualify as a baby? Jess was unsure. She had heard the arguments for both sides of the termination case and now that she had lost the little life growing inside her she felt that it had to indeed qualify. She felt a tear trickle down her cheek. The doctor had told her she would be tearful and emotional, and she had been given an appointment for next week with a bereavement and baby-loss counsellor. She hadn't thought that to be necessary yesterday, but sitting here now, she was glad that she had let them arrange it for her. She plunged her hand back into the popcorn bag and took out a fistful stuffing it unashamedly into her mouth. She felt happy all of a sudden. She wondered what Nate would say if he could see her right at this moment. He had popped out briefly to do a small photography session for a newborn. He had skirted round telling her about it for fear that she would be upset but she had assured him she was Ok, and that life had to move on. Did she really think that ? Was she ready to think that ?

With a sigh she lay back on the couch and picked up the remote control. Time for a thrilling binge watch she decided.

Pittenweem   July 2021

CHAPTER SIXTY

Maybeth was sitting at the bench at the harbour. She was due to meet Davy and

Avril in an hour. She had so much to think about. What would this reunion really do? Who was it really for? Would it cause more harm than good? Would her mother flee again? As she sat, she noticed a young girl heading towards her. As she got closer, she realized it was the girl from the estate agents. The girl had a sad expression in her eyes. Perfectly understandable, Maybeth thought. The girl approached and signaled to the space on the bench next to Maybeth.

'Do you mind if I sit down there?' the girl asked sadly.

'Of course not,' Maybeth answered putting on her mask, ' I'll budge up a bit and give you a little more space.'

' I keep forgetting about the social distance. I just need to sit down.'

Maybeth moved along, but the girl was so slight that she would have been far enough away where she was. Ok maybe not two meters, but far enough and both women were masked.

'You're the girl from the Estate Agents, aren't you?' Maybeth asked.

The girl nodded. ' Yes, I'm Kirsten.'

'Maybeth' Maybeth said.

The girl nodded again. ' I remember' she replied.

'I'm really sorry about Mark' Maybeth said looking at her.

Kirsten looked out onto the water. Maybeth could see her eyes had started to mist.

'So am I,' she croaked, her voice thickening with emotion, ' he was such a nice person and a great boss, he was really encouraging and…' Kirsten tailed off and she started to sob gently. ' I'm sorry. I can't seem to stop crying.'

Maybeth checked in her pockets and found a packet of paper tissues. She remembered from her brownie days to be prepared and these days she always carried a packet with her along with a safety pin and a clean pair of pants. She didn't think the pants were a brownie thing. That perhaps came later during her late teens when she and Nuala had been involved in the club scene. They had loved the clubs just off Piccadilly in London and when they had time, between studies, they would have some amazing nights, dancing and sweating and laughing and sometimes not going home at the same time. She smiled as she passed the hankies to Kirsten.

'Keep them.' Kirsten took out a tissue, removed her mask and blew her nose. Returning her mask, she put both the used tissue and the packet into her pocket.

'Do you know when the funeral will be?'

'I think next week. His sister is dealing with everything. She called me yesterday.' Kirsten sniffed 'the shop is shut today and tomorrow until they get someone in.'

Maybeth looked at Kirsten, she was distraught. She made the decision in that moment to tell her what she had just at that moment decided.

'I'm staying. I'll be there.' She blurted. The ferocity with which she answered startled even herself.

'Really?' Kirsten asked, instantly brighter.

Maybeth nodded, shocked by what she had just done. What else was to be done? The girl had been so sad, and Maybeth had felt the urge to do what she could to stop the sadness, or at least ease it anyway. She would stay.

'Not forever,' she clarified for both of them, ' until they find a replacement.'

Maybeth had a sudden image of one of her favourite characters from childhood, *Mary Poppins*. One of her favourite lines from that film had been something about staying only until the wind changed. She had almost laughed as she imagined herself flying over the harbour with a bird handled umbrella and her feet at right angles. She looked at Kirsten and saw that she was deep in thought. She had to break the moment.

' I need to go. I've got a dinner date in about forty minutes and I have to change and freshen up.' She rose and stretched. Kirsten stood up too.

'Anyone nice?' Kirsten asked teasingly.

Maybeth liked this girl. She could see that it would be pleasant to work with her.

'My dad.' She said, smiling.

'Lovely.' Kirsten replied, although a little disappointed that there would be no gossip of a mystery man or woman. ' Thanks for letting me sit with you.'

Maybeth nodded slowly ' and thanks for...sitting with me.' They shared a short laugh.

'See you not tomorrow but the next day.' Kirsten said as she started to walk away. Maybeth paused briefly before she responded ' Yes, see you then.'

When she had told Laura she would help out she hadn't felt the need that she was feeling now, to stay here. She watched Kirsten walk away. She looked happier and there was definitely a slight skip in her step now that hadn't been there on her approach. She looked at her watch and headed back to the Old Chandlery to get ready. She would pack tomorrow and move to Julie and Ronnie's, but for now she had to get ready to play the little matchmaker.

Pittenweem   Jluy 2021

CHAPTER SIXTY-ONE

'Oh my days! I think I know your dad' Debbie shouted with a sparkle in her eyes as Davy entered the café. ' Look at you! Davy, you look about twenty years younger.'

Davy grinned. He felt good and he was glad that other people could see it too. He had been to the barbers and had gone for a slightly shorter cut. He still had quite thick hair, so he wasn't shy about losing any. With his new jeans, shirt and shoes he felt more stylish than he ever had in his life. Clothes had always only ever been a practicality for him but today Davy felt good. He had arrived a little early but that had been his plan. He liked a certain booth in here and wanted to make sure that he got it. There it was. Empty and inviting him in. He removed his jacket and hung it on the coat hook on the wall and walked over to the booth. He sat on the left side in at the wall. He liked a wall seat. The table was set for the standard four. It was only himself and Maybeth who were eating and he wondered if he should get Debbie to remove the spare cutlery and napkins.

There were two customers in apart from himself. As he looked around he noticed that there was a reserved sign on a table with a large balloon saying "Happy Anniversary" in pink and silver lettering. Davy smiled but he also felt a sadness for whoever was celebrating. The celebrations would be limited to a very small number. This Covid pandemic was certainly changing everything. People were no longer free to be out with or eat with families unless it was in groups of six or four in public eateries. Debbie's business must be suffering. Davy had made quite a bit of money over the years and always left a bit extra in his tip when he paid his bill. He was grateful to Debbie and this place. Debbie always made him feel welcome and now that Maybeth was here, he had more company to talk to. He had been a bit lonely he now realised. He didn't want to think about what would happen when Maybeth left. She would be gone soon. He shook that thought away. Outside the café he saw her pass the window to enter, but she wasn't alone.

Pittenweem   July 2021

CHAPTER SIXTY-TWO

Avril had sat in her car at the harbour side waiting to catch Maybeth. She didn't want to go into the café alone. She had driven over early so that she could look out on to the once familiar waters. She looked at her bench. The bench that could tell a thousand tales. The bench that held a thousand secrets in its wood. And there was the boat. The *Betty Smith.* Davy's first crew job as a paid fisherman had been aboard this trawler. In 1993. The year her life had changed. She looked at the chipped paint and the rusting chains. This boat had been almost new back then and the men had been proud to work on it. Davy hadn't been able to stop himself talking about it. She sighed and felt a bit queasy, looking up she noticed a figure coming out of the Chandlery . Her old house. This was another eerie coincidence that her daughter who had lived inside her when she lived inside that building was now an adult staying in that same place. The figure was Maybeth, Avril noticed.

She got out of the car and shouted her name. Maybeth looked up and smiled. She waited for Avril to lock the car and join her.

'I was a wee bit early,' Avril explained 'I'm always a wee bit early.'' Me too' Maybeth admitted ' It must be in the genes.'

Avril felt a warmth clamber up her body and nestle at her heart. Maybeth was acknowledging an attachment.

'This place hasn't changed much, ' Avril mused ' the same boats, the same paintwork and the same curtains up in the window above the café.' she giggled.

'Really? Maybeth laughed

'No, I'm joking, I'm pretty sure the ones in there were orange back then.'

Maybeth grimaced. She took her mask from her pocket and placed it on her face. Avril did the same with her own.

'Shall we go and eat?' Maybeth said as they walked towards the café.

Pittenweem   July 2021

CHAPTER SIXTY-THREE

He was staring at the doorway, and he couldn't quite believe what he was seeing. There was Avril walking towards him behind their daughter.

Maybeth had set this up. Davy had known he would have to face this moment at some time but it was now here sooner than he would have liked. He stood up as they approached the table. Avril looked just as stunned as he, although he could only see her eyes peering over her mask. Those eyes he could remember. The greenish blue of her irises and a soft yellow rim. So unusual yet so familiar to him. Her hair was hanging loose around her face. She had always worn it tied back when she was young. She was looking at him too. Taking in his thick hair. His eyes looked older. The crinkles around them showing her that he was a happy man. He was smiling under his mask and his eyes sparkled. Maybeth and Avril reached the table and Maybeth spoke.

'I've brought someone to see you.'

No preamble, no warning. Davy recognized this now as Maybeth's way. She was direct, that was for sure. She stood there and he could tell that she was grinning too. He could hear it on her voice and there was a very obvious look of mischief in her eyes.

'Avril,' Davy heard himself say ' please, have a seat. It's so good to see you.'

Avril took the seat across from him and Maybeth sat beside her facing the empty chair. Avril had a brief thought that Maybeth had sat beside her deliberately to stop her running away again. It was finally time to face up to Davy and put her demons to rest. Debbie rushed over at that moment to take their jackets. She was unusually quiet as she took them but whispered to Maybeth, asking her to fill her in later. Maybeth had nodded and Debbie put the jackets over her arm and left.

'So here we are.' Maybeth said removing her mask.

Avril and Davy followed suit and then sat silently. Davy looking at Avril as if he couldn't quite believe she was here and Avril looking at her fingers, then Avril spoke, tentatively.

'How are you Davy?'

'I'm well. You?'

Avril nodded and answered in the affirmative.

'Isn't it great that Maybeth found us? Davy gushed, unable now to stop himself ' I was so shocked when I saw her, but really glad because I haven't stopped wondering and thinking about you both since the day you disappeared. Why did you disappear?

It was out before he could stop himself. Now he knew where Maybeth got her forthrightness from. Avril's face changed and he saw her brow go down fleetingly. She had done this a lot when she was young when she hadn't liked what was being said to her. Avril managed to catch herself. She had been expecting this at some point in her life. She had gone over this scene in her head for years. This eventual showdown, but this was without their daughter being present. This was a time when they still didn't know where she was. Avril had visualized herself coming back here one day and finding Davy so that they could perhaps look for her together, but, here they were sitting with her and about to have this conversation. Debbie chose the moment to come back and take a drinks order. Maybeth asked for a sprite, Davy chose black coffee. There was still a no alcohol law due to the guidelines and this was the heaviest drink he could think of. Avril had continued to sit quietly only ordering a full fat coke, no ice, in a soft voice when Debbie looked at her. She had continued to look at Davy. Davy had flicked his gaze nervously between Avril and Maybeth. Had he gone too early? No. He had waited years for an explanation. Avril needed to tell him why she had gone. He suddenly felt angry. An anger that he had not felt since she had left. He couldn't look at her for a moment. The feelings he had right now were too intense. Maybeth's voice broke through his conflicting emotions.

'Maybe we could eat first and answer the big questions later, what do you think?'

The tone held a warning in it. Maybeth was right, but she had initiated this meeting with no warning to Davy or Avril, judging by the looks he was getting from her. Davy shimmied over to the outer seat and stood up.

'Excuse me, ' he muttered ' I have to use the toilet.'

When he was out of sight Avril let out the breath, she hadn't known she was holding. Maybeth turned to look at her.

'I didn't really think this through, did I? Listen, I'm going to leave you two to talk.' She stood.

'No, you don't need too go' Avril put her hand on Maybeth's arm.

'I won't leave the café. I'll go over and sit with Debbie and wait until you two have spoken. Even if it takes a while. Just let me know when you want me to come back.' Maybeth removed Avril's arm gently and tapped it affirmingly. ' This needs to happen without me.'

Debbie was returning with the tray of drinks. Maybeth lifted her sprite and explained to Debbie that she was leaving the table for a bit. She tucked herself at the corner of the counter just out of eyeline. Debbie would be able to give her a running commentary about what was happening from the other side of the bar if she so desired to know. When Davy returned from the toilet he stopped and looked around before he sat down. He looked anxiously at Avril.

'Where's Maybeth?'

'She's giving us some talking time Davy. So please, let's just talk. I need to explain.' An hour later they were still talking. Debbie had taken over some olives and bread and a carafe of water to tide them over and refilled their drinks too. The food was lying untouched, but the conversation was still flowing. They had cried and there had been some laughter too, although faces had been mostly solemn, and they were really listening to each other. Debbie had been great at keeping Maybeth up to speed. Speaking in a low whisper as she passed her. Maybeth had been playing on her phone the entire time. She had sent a text to Laura and another with funny gifs to Nuala and had received some back. She had also managed to find out that nurses pay down in England was ready to fall another 7% and that the Tokyo Olympics that was supposed to go ahead in 2020 was finishing up and had been a great success by all accounts. She usually read the news every day but since arriving in Scotland it hadn't seemed as important to keep up with it. Maybeth looked up from her phone just in time to see Avril signaling to her to come back to the table. Maybeth put her phone back off and walked over.

'Good timing' Debbie shouted ' you all look starving.' The mood was certainly lighter as Maybeth sat down, but she could see that Davy looked worn out. The sparkle in his eyes had dulled down and it was obvious that he had been crying hard. They were still red and watery looking. Avril looked different and somehow, they both seemed more relaxed. Maybeth had read books about people's personalities and even their looks changing after a sadness or worry had been lifted from their life, and today she was actually witnessing it firsthand. They both looked younger and with their masks removed she could see genuine smiles on their faces. They were smiling at each other. Maybeth could see the love that had once so obviously been there, and she was certain it was there still. She stopped the thought and warned herself not to go there. She had to let them work this thing out on their own. She had been the product of their love and if it was to be, it would be. She began humming to herself *Que Sera* as Debbie took the order. Maybeth and Davy both chose the crab and lemon butter risotto and Avril went for the scampi and chili fries.

'Thank you Maybeth' Avril said, with a voice stronger than Maybeth had ever heard her use.

'Yes,' Davy added ' We needed that.' Maybeth smiled at them both.

'I know' she grinned ' Now, once we've eaten I'm going to let you tell me what it was like growing up.' Avril and Davy shared a look and both of them started to laugh. Davy nodded. 'That we can do.'

The food arrived and they ate in silence. Each of them lost in their own thoughts. Each lighter than they had been when they had walked in. each happier than they had ever felt.

Pittenweem   July 2021

CHAPTER SIXTY-FOUR

They had talked. Avril had started off, telling Davy about the day that she had left. She had shared with him how she had felt when he had dismissed her. He apologised and explained that he had been a confused and frightened young boy who had no experience with anything to do with babies. They had argued lightly back and forward. Avril had been young and frightened too. She had actually seen and held the baby with the knowledge that she couldn't keep her. Davy had asked her why she had named her Maybeth and then he had thanked her for it. If Avril hadn't had done that, they would never have known who she was. Avril was happy that she had had the foresight. They spoke about Davy's life after. His years away from the shore, about the deaths of his mum and dad and then his twin sister Davina's illness and subsequent passing last year. Avril was sorry to learn about Davina's death. They had been friends. Davy said that the pain he had felt losing them had been a pain that he had carried every day since Avril had left. He had felt as if he was in perpetual mourning. He told her that he had missed her every day.

Avril had teared up too and apologised again. They had spoken about what might have been. How they could have perhaps kept the baby, but, given Davy's mum and dad's strict presbyterian ways they might never have acknowledged the baby. Davy and Avril both agreed now looking at the amazing woman Maybeth had grown up to be, that they had done the right thing. This had led to resolution and a rebuilding. They had spoken about this place. The changes that had taken place, like the new community hub and the things that would never change. The harbour smells and noises. Avril told Davy about her family , about Chris and her journey to this point. He was genuinely interested. She could see it in his eyes. She could see the pleasure in them that she remembered from when they were growing up and she was telling him something. He always looked fascinated in what she had to say. She would be excited sharing stories and he would act her enthusiasm out with the widening and closing up of his eyes. This used to make her laugh. She wanted to laugh now, she felt so much joy right here in this moment. A wound was healed, and her only disappointment was that she had not had the courage to have done this sooner. Watching Davy and Maybeth chatter freely now was the icing on her cake. This was the moment that surpassed the moment she had been waiting for all of her life. She felt the heavy shackles of fear, guilt, sadness and hurt dropping from her and a lightness, a goodness and the happiness of freedom wrapping and comfortably settling around her like nothing she had ever felt before.

Pittenweem   July 2021

CHAPTER SIXTY-FIVE

Davy couldn't take his eyes from her face. Avril was still talking, and he was drinking in every word. She was, yet somehow wasn't the Avril he knew. Yes, she still sounded the same and had the same laugh and cadence in her speech, but she was a woman now. She looked a lot like her Aunty Morag. Davy had remembered to ask about Aunty Morag. She was the greatest influence in Avril's teenage years. Aunty Morag was the person that Avril had run to. She had gone from here and done lots with her life and Davy had despised her when Avril left. Blaming Morag for taking Avril away from him. His young selfish brain had blamed everyone but himself. He had listened to Avril explain why she had had to go, and he had said sorry at least a dozen times. He was sorry for everything. Now that they had spoken Davy was just so glad that they were all together. After they had eaten, they had all talked some more. Davy told them about the shore walks and how Avril and he had stuffed two crabs in the minister's wife's handbag during Sunday school one day and one had pinched her hand. They had blamed someone else for it, they couldn't remember who, but they had still got into trouble for it. Avril regaled them with tales of hiding behind people at the busy bus stop so that they could sneak on the bus for free and go to the nearest town on a Saturday afternoon, the times they were chased by the bull at the farm on the hill when they were taking a shortcut by crossing the field and reading to Mrs. Murray who was blind on a Tuesday evening at six o'clock. Avril had loved reading and Davy enjoyed listening to the classics being read. He remembered some of the characters still. Mrs. Peggoty, Long John Silver and Anne Shirley of Green Gables. Maybeth listened and watched as they reconnected. Her parents. Where she had first began. She looked at her watch now. It was after ten. Debbie had seen off the rest of her customers a while ago. She signaled to Debbie to ready the bill.

'I think we need to make a move. Debbie needs to close up' Maybeth announced gently. Avril and Davy seemed reluctant to move.

'You could always come to mine for a coffee' Davy invited.

Avril smiled. ' Maybe another time, I have to get back.'

Davy nodded.

'I'll give you my number and we can arrange for me to come back through again soon.' Avril continued, blushing.

Davy bit back a smile and Maybeth looked down at her feet. She felt like a gooseberry. She took a piece of paper and a pen from her handbag and handed it to Avril who jotted down her number and handed it to Davy.

'I'll see you soon Maybeth?' Avril questioned hopefully.

'Definitely, I'm starting work here the day after tomorrow, but I'll have Sunday's off.'

'So why don't you both come through to mine next Sunday for your lunch? Avril suggested. Davy and Maybeth shared a look and nodded.

'It's a date.' Maybeth said as she watched the pair of them fluster. They said the goodbyes and Avril drove away. Maybeth said goodnight to Davy and watched him walk home. He definitely looked taller, and his stride was that of a much younger man. Maybeth giggled to herself, Debbie looked out of the café door.

'Is the coast clear?' she whispered.

Maybeth nodded.

'Right, get back in here. I have a fine malt and a lock in. I want to hear all the details and I'm not taking no for an answer. Maybeth shook her head playfully. 'Well, when you put it like that…' she said stepping back inside to the darkness of the now unlit café. Debbie bolted the door, and they made their way through to the back office. Debbie opened the bottle of malt whisky and poured a measure for Maybeth and opened a can of coke for herself. She was driving and didn't mind playing host.

'Right, spill.' she commanded in jest and spill Maybeth did without leaving out any detail.

Pittenween   July 2021

CHAPTER SIXTY-SIX

Maybeth had so much to tell Laura. She called her the next morning to fill her in and to get the information she needed to start in the office in the morning. It was Mark's funeral today and Debbie and Charlie were going from the café. Charlie loved a purvey he had told her, which had taken her aback. Debbie assured her that plenty of the older generation went to funerals of people they hardly knew just for a good feed. She even knew of a man who had three black ties and scoured the obituary pages in the local newspapers and would turn up at funerals where he didn't know the deceased just so that he could get a free drink at the wake. Laura had asked question upon question regarding her parents meet up. She particularly wanted to know how they had looked when they first set eyes on each other.

'For goodness' sake Laura, you've asked me three times,' Maybeth chided.

'I need to know, its the romantic in me,' Laura groaned, 'it's the romantic in me.' Maybeth had rolled her eyes. Laura had met someone. Again. And it was love at first sight. Again. His name was Keith, and he was a carpenter who had done some work on a property they had been selling. It had just so happened that Laura was there every time he was. They had been on two dates, and she loved him or so she said. Maybeth was so used to Laura being in love and was happy for her and on this occasion, she was equally happy for herself being miles away from it when it all went disastrously wrong and started to untangle. The last Mr. Right had been Mr. Wrong Brand of Trainers and Laura had ended it by text and spent a week crying that she would be single forever. Maybeth had had to console and cajole her until she met someone else. Maybeth spent the day cleaning up and packing for her move to Julie and Ronnie's house this evening. She had paid up the Old Chandlery bill and was giving it a once over, checking that was no stray biscuit packet or sock under the bed. She liked this place. She ran her hand over the cold stone of the bare wall. Her mum had lived in this very place. She had been in her mum's womb in this very room, Maybeth went to the window seat and sat looking out at the harbour. She thought about the events of the past weeks. She had achieved more and met more people in this short time than she had since starting work. She called her parents down south and filled them in on all that had happened. She told them about her birth mother and father meeting. Her mum had thought it was quite romantic too. Her dad just thought it was nice. He was such a placid man who liked nothing better than to potter round a garden centre looking for seeds. He was on his way there now he told her before they said goodbye. Maybeth gave the rooms a final look over and lifted her bags out to the car. She posted the key through the letter box as she had been asked to do and got into the car. She turned and looked again at the building she had called home for a couple of weeks and smiled. From the outside she could tell that her mum's secret hadn't been the only one that it had kept. This house was full of mystery. She smiled again silently and made her way to her grand-parent's house.

Edinburgh   July 2021

CHAPTER SIXTY-SEVEN

Sophie was dancing around the living room to *George Ezra's Shotgun*. She was supposed to be helping Avril to tidy. It was Sunday morning and Maybeth and Davy were coming today.

'Sophie, can you stop spinning for a minute?' Avril scolded. ' You're meant to be emptying the wastepaper basket.'

Sophie giggled and stretched her body down towards the bin. ' I can multitask,' she said 'I can stretch and point and twirl and tidy.' She demonstrated every action as she spoke. She was so excited. Avril had told her everything that had happened when she met Davy and she couldn't wait to meet him and more importantly se Maybeth again. She was over the moon that Maybeth was staying at her gran and grandpa's house too. Nate and Jess were coming later, and Avril had wondered if Davy might feel a little bit ambushed, but this was her world and he had agreed to come into it. She was feeling quite giddy. Her oldest daughter was coming here with her dad. This was huge. She looked at Sophie who was now sitting scrolling through her phone. It was difficult to believe that Avril had had a life before Nate and Sophie. Davy and Maybeth were from that life, and they were going to merge into this life today. She felt the nerves starting to bubble. She looked at the clock on the wall and once around the room. It was tidy.

'Mum, stop fussing,' Sophie said, one eye on her phone and one on her mum. Ever since she was little Sophie had always looked out for her mum and today was no different. 'Let me make us a cuppa and we can keep you distracted until they come. We could play *Jenga* or something.'

Avril started to laugh this was always Sophie's go to when she needed entertained. She really was a tonic this girl, Avril thought.

'Yes to the tea but I'll pass on the *Jenga*.' Avril answered as they walked into the kitchen.

Pittenweem   July 2021

CHAPTER SIXTY-EIGHT

Maybeth was waiting in the car for Davy. It had been a busy week. She had started work. It had taken her a fair, few hours to go through Mark's set ups and it had felt horrible sitting at a dead man's desk. His presence was everywhere. There was a half-finished mars bar on the desk and Maybeth could see the teeth marks. Kirsten was a great help but had burst into tears at times. She had kept Laura up to speed through emails and she felt better being kept going. The view from the office window was also a lot more pleasant than the one she had in central London, and she hadn't had to queue for a sandwich wasting a full lunchtime in one of the cities thousands of delis. Not here. Here, Kirsten ran to Debbie's café and within five minutes was back with a soup or a sandwich or both on one particularly trying day this week. Davy appeared and raised his hand in a shy wave. He looked great. The car journey passed quickly. Maybeth wasn't speeding but they had chatted non-stop. Davy was like an excited child who had never seen the world. He looked out of the window as a passenger this time. The last time he and Maybeth had been out he had driven. He spent the journey pointing out places and sharing stories of things happening here or over there. They arrived at the address Avril had sent and it looked nice. Avril had kept to her word and bought Chris out. She loved this house. They rang the doorbell and waited all of two seconds before the door was flung wide open and Sophie burst out into Maybeth's arms with a delighted squeal.

'Hey sis,' she yelled, laughing and jumping around. Davy hoped against hope that he wouldn't be treated to the same greeting. He needn't have worried. Once Sophie had calmed down, she led them into the living room where Avril was waiting with Nate and Jess. They had arrived earlier. Jess was feeling much better and had gone back to work. The chat with the therapist had been just what she had needed, and she had left the decision up to Jess to keep in touch or not. Just having the woman's number had been comfort enough.

Avril was standing as they entered.

'Hello,' she said ' come on in. It's lovely to see you both.'

Davy and Maybeth came in and sat down on the two armchairs as directed. Nate and Jess were on the sofa, Avril had brought a chair in from the dining area and Sophie sat in front of the huge television screen that sat in the corner at an angle.

'I'll get us all a drink,' Avril bustled. 'Tea? Coffee?'

"I'd love a coffee.' Davy answered almost immediately. His voice boomed in the smaller space. Maybeth hadn't realised how loud his voice was. It was probably trained to be that loud from when he was out at sea. He would need to be heard over the noise of the gulls and the boat engines. Avril, on the other hand remembered it well. She took the order and walked into the kitchen. She felt like an over-excited teenager. She still loved him she realised. Where had that come from? That thought had come out of nowhere. Her heart hammered and she stood for a moment and looked out of the window. Someone entered the kitchen, and she caught the shadow through the glass.

'Need a hand?' It was Maybeth. Avril turned and Maybeth's brow furrowed in concern. ' Are you OK?'

'Y.Yes I'm fine,' Avril stammered breaking from her reverie.

"It must be quite a shock for you having Davy and me here.'

'It's lovely," Avril answered.

'Is he still as you remember him?' Maybeth asked gently. Avril turned to her daughter 'and more' she blurted and then her eyes widened with shock. What was she saying? Maybeth put her hand to her mouth and her eyes widened to match her mother's. She still had her mask on, but she was smiling widely underneath. 'Mother, I do believe you're blushing' Maybeth teased. Avril shushed her.

'Oh Maybeth, I was standing making tea and I heard the big voice and realised that I still had feelings for him. Please don't say anything' Avril pleaded. Maybeth stood beside Avril as they silently looked out of the window and put her arm around her shoulder. 'My lips are sealed.' She replied.

Pittenweem   2021 (Christmas Eve)

CHAPTER SIXTY-NINE

It was early morning and Davy was out on the *Betty Smith*. He had taken her out to check the lobster pots. Letting the engine idle, he lifted the wooden and rope bound traps out of the water and checked his catch. He had caught a few nice sized lobster in there. He hauled them on deck and piled them at the bow of the boat. The air was fresh, and the weather was mild for this time of year. It was Christmas Eve. Just more than four months since he had been reunited with Avril again. Things were good between them. He had chatted to her on the phone almost every evening and they had met up a few times, with and without Maybeth. He had been invited to Julie and Ronnie's for Christmas lunch tomorrow. It was the first proper Christmas he had had in years. When Davina was alive, they would go to a restaurant and have the set meal. It was nice enough, but he missed the clamour and chat of childhood Christmases with all the family. Yes, he was really looking forward to the day. He had bought presents for everyone too. Maybeth had helped his choose some lovely gifts. He had found a beautiful handmade jewellery store along the coast and had bought three nice necklaces for Jess, Sophie and Avril. He had also sneakily bought a bracelet for Maybeth with an amber stone setting. She had been browsing another section of the shop and he had caught the owners attention. They had performed a crazy eyebrow and hand signal mime to get the message across that the gift was for Maybeth and she must not know. The owner had wrapped up the gifts beautifully. He had also bought presents for Ronnie and Julie. (A garden ornament that Julie had spoken about wanting last week). Nate got a tie and he had bought Debbie a bottle of perfume that Maybeth had managed to order online from *Jo Malone*. Davy had never heard of him, but knew it was good as it had been quite dear. He didn't mind what the cost was, Debbie had helped him get to know Maybeth and he would be forever grateful. They were meeting up with Debbie this evening at the café for a small twilight supper. Due to Covid there were only so many allowed still at any gathering. Maybeth had helped to organize it.

Davy felt that he was relying on Maybeth. She was enjoying her work here and had made no mention of leaving and going back down south, but he always worried that one day she would go. He felt sadness start to fall on him as he stood on the boat now. Giving himself a shake, he started the engine, turned the boat and headed back to shore. He loved this life. He loved this boat. He would head back home and have his shower once the pots had been weighed and the payment had been made by the harbourmaster. Davy had made a lot of money from these waters. As he came into the harbour he looked towards the bench. Avril was sitting there. He rubbed his eyes, surely it was his imagination. No, she was still there when he took his hands away. Something was wrong. What was she doing here so early in the morning?

Pittenweem   (Christmas Eve) 2021

CHAPTER SEVENTY

She hadn't been able to sleep. She had thought it was heartburn but after taking some *Rennie's* and milk it still hadn't eased. She was climbing back upstairs to bed when she collapsed. Maybeth had heard the thump and woke up. She was a light sleeper at the best of times. She threw back the quilt and reached for her dressing gown. She heard Julie and Ronnie's bedroom door open, and she opened hers a fraction of a second later. Julie was lying on the stairs as if she was asleep. Ronnie was leaning over her frantically searching for a pulse and calling her name. Maybeth ran back into her room and picked up her phone. She dialed for an ambulance and then called Avril. Ronnie had carefully lifted Julie to the bottom of the stairs and was performing CPR. Tears were streaming down his face as he methodically kept up the rhythm as if not only Julie's, but his life depended on it. The ambulance arrived quickly. Maybeth was always astonished at the speed at which things were done up here. The NHS system seemed to work better here than in England. The paramedics worked quickly, and Julie and Ronnie left in the ambulance. Julie had suffered a massive heart attack or so the paramedics thought She was still alert which was a good sign and they would continue to do what they could. Ronnie had been ashen faced and silent. It had just gone one thirty in the morning. Maybeth squeezed his arm as he passed her, and he returned a very faint smile. Now, she was alone. She walked to the kitchen and switched on the kettle. Avril was on her way to the hospital and said she would keep her updated. For now Maybeth had to sit tight and wait for news.

Pittenweem   (Christmas Eve) 2021

CHAPTER SEVENTY-ONE

Davy stepped off the boat, finished his work and walked towards the bench. Avril hadn't moved. She heard his feet on the path and turned to look at him. She looked so sad and pale. Davy's heart quickened. Why was she here? Early in the morning on Christmas Eve in the cold.

'What's happened?' he asked as he reached her and sat down beside her. He was facing her and the care and worry in his voice sent Avril into floods of tears.

"It's Mum' Avril wept. 'She's had a heart attack.'

'Is she OK?' Davy asked.

'Yes, Dad saved her they said,' Avril answered, more in control of herself. 'He did CPR before the ambulance got there. She'll be in hospital for a while, but they've got her on a monitor, and they are pretty certain that she will recover with rest.' Avril moved the hair that had blown into her face and continued.

'they had originally thought it was a massive attack, but they don't think so now, but...' Avril stopped talking. Davy moved over on the bench and put his arm around her. They were both facing out to the water now. Avril leant into Davy. She fitted perfectly, her head in the join between arm and shoulder. He smelled of the sea and the fish, but it was a smell that she remembered well, and it filled her with a sudden calmness. She closed her eyes and let the silence within settle as she concentrated on other sounds without. Davy's heartbeat, the gulls, the wind now starting to whip. She suddenly felt cold. Davy felt her shiver.

'Come on, let's go to mine for a hot drink and a sit by the fire.' She let him help her to stand and they walked the short distance to his house.

'Where's your car parked?' Davy asked not seeing a car parked near where they had been.

'I left it at Mum and Dad's. When I got back from the hospital with Dad, he and Maybeth went to bed. I knew I wouldn't sleep so I just walked down here.'

Davy looked at his watch. It was eight minutes past nine.

'What time did it happen?' He asked.

"Around one this morning, Dad and Maybeth found her on the stairs. I arrived at the hospital about three and they had stabilised her.' She yawned quietly. ' I'm going back at lunchtime with dad.'

They reached the cottage and Davy opened the door. It was warm inside and Avril felt it immediately thawing her icy cold face and hands.

'Take your coat off and have a seat. I'll make us some tea.' Davy said as he shucked off his own jacket and gloves and made his way into the kitchen. Avril sat down. The couch was comfy. She rested her head on the soft arm and fell instantly to sleep. Davy popped his head out of the door and smiled as he saw her. He took a blanket from his bedroom wardrobe and laid it softly over her. The tea would wait he thought as he made his way for a shower. Tiptoeing quietly through and away from her in order to give Avril her rest.

St Andrew's Hospital   (Christmas Eve) 2021

CHAPTER SEVENTY-TWO

Ronnie and Avril sat together behind their masks as the steady beep of the machine monitoring Julie's heartbeat sounded loudly in the barren hospital room. Julie was awake now but groggy. It was quarter past four and Sophie and Nate were out in the car park. They had been refused permission due to the restrictions and Sophie had said she wasn't leaving the grounds. Nate had driven Jess back to Ronnie and Julie's house in an hour round trip and was now letting Sophie sit in the car with him. Julie was in bed making sure that Ronnie knew what was to happen tomorrow.

' There are tins of soup. Avril will see to the turkey and main. Get Nate to buy some nice wine and Sophie can serve the trifle. I bought two yesterday and they are in the fridge.'

Ronnie smiled and rolled his eyes. Here Julie was lying in a hospital bed and still arranging and organizing life for everyone. He felt tears come to his eyes.

'And don't you cry, I'm still here.' She scolded weakly.

'Thank God for that.' Ronnie replied raising her hand to his lips. He wasn't a particularly religious man, but he had prayed more in the past twenty-four hours than he ever had done. Maybe there was something in it after all. He would nip into the church tomorrow to say a wee thank you. There was a ten o'clock Christmas morning service. A flyer had been pushed through the letterbox last week.

'Now, I'm alright here so please don't worry about me and I'll be angry if you don't have a good time.' Julie looked sternly at them both. Avril started to giggle.

"Oh mum," she said.

'Now away home and start prepping for tomorrow.' Ronnie and Avril stood up. They could see that Julie was tired. The nurse was bustling around and nodded to them both. 'You can come back tomorrow.' She said.

"I'll be here for twelve. I have to be back in the house for two.' Ronnie said quietly.

'Anything to get out of the kitchen.' Julie muttered sleepily ''See you tomorrow loves.' She added.

'I'll come on boxing day.' Avril added ' and I'll bring Sophie, if that's OK otherwise she'll go ninja?

'Two visitors only.' The nurse said and make sure she is masked and you've taken a Covid test before you come please.'

'Love you Mum,' Avril whispered looking down, but Julie was already asleep.

Pittenweem   (Christmas Day) 2021

CHAPTER SEVENTY-TWO

Ronnie, Avril and Maybeth crunched down the gravel path away from the church. Maybeth had wanted to go with Ronnie purely on a mission to see where she had been left by her mother. Avril had held on to her tightly as she showed her, for fear that she would lose her again. The service had been very short. The church had been allowed to open but no one could sit together; no music was allowed or carols to be sung and everyone had to leave by a different exit than when they arrived. Instead of the smell of Christmas and spice, today the church had smelled of sanitizing gel. Nevertheless, the minister and her team had done a lovely job with the decorations. They made their way back up to the house. Avril had put the turkey in the oven to cook before she left, Sophie had been instructed to peel the potatoes and prep and clean the veg, Nate was laying the table and Jess was wrapping presents. They had arrived this morning early with bags and boxes. The house was in chaos as they opened the door. Happy chaos. Sophie had found a Christmas playlist on her phone and the singing, although not entirely tuneful, was accompanying the industrious atmosphere. Aunty Morag had arrived too. She was going to the hospital with Ronnie. Avril had had a difficult conversation with Aunty Morag when Maybeth had been found and things were almost back to a firm footing between them. Aunty Morag had been upset that Avril had spent all that time with her and had been so close, yet didn't feel able to share. After meeting Maybeth, however, the upset hadn't lasted and Aunty Morag welcomed Maybeth as she did Nate and Sophie. After a quick sandwich Ronnie and Morag left. Maybeth and Avril slotted in with the prep and soon everything was under control. Nate poured everyone a Bucks Fizz and they sat down for five minutes to watch the tail end of *The Snowman* for the umpteenth time.

Just before three Ronnie returned with Davy. He had just got out of his car when Ronnie pulled up. They had exchanged Christmas greetings. Davy had been a bit worried about coming. He thought the rule about only family gathering together and minimizing contact would mean he couldn't be here, but he had taken a test (negative) this morning and would stay a distance from everyone with his mask on until he ate. He had shared his concern with Maybeth who said he was her family and she wanted him there too. They had spaced everything out and left the windows open. It was a cold day and blizzards had been forecast although nothing had come yet. The meal went well with everyone eating more than they ought. As they shared in a glas of port Avril began to clear the table.

'Leave it, Mum.' Nate said.

'You know she won't,' Sophie responded. ' She always does this. It's the OCD.'

They all laughed.

'I'll help.' Davys said rising from his seat.

'You don't need to.' Avril said.

'I know I don't need to, that's why I offered,' he answered, winking at Sophie.

He moved around the the table and started to stack the empty puidding plates. Jess had made a huge Christmas pudding with brandy butter. It was delicious and with Sophie insisting they had to eat the trifle that Mum had bought they were all now fit too burst. Ronnie raised a glass. ' A toast.' Everyone stopped and raised their glasses. Avril and Davy raised empty wine bottles and laughed.

'To family,' he declared loudly. 'To those who are far away,' he looked at Maybeth who he knew would be thinking of her parents down south. She had called them this morning and was going to see them on New Years Eve.

' ...and those we wish were here now instead of in the hospital.' Sophie shouted.

'To new found family.' Davy added

'...and all the generations here today.' Ronnie finished.

'To family.' They all shouted as they drank their toast.

Something called *The Masked Singer* had just started on the TV and Sophie and Nate were laughing about someone being dressed as a sausage.

'How embarrassing,' Nate was saying. ' How desperate would you have to want to be famous to dress up as a sausage and go on national television.' Jess laughed.

'But they're already famous,' said Sophie. "Don't you know anything?' she cheekily teased.

In the kitchen, Avril smiled. This was the way she liked it. Nate and Sophie bickering, everyone well fed and contented. She missed her mum but knew that she was being well looked after. Davy and

Avril had settled into a system. She was washing the dishes and he was drying. Ronnie and Julie had a dishwasher, but Avril always liked peace on Christmas Day.

'I've missed you.' Davy said looking at Avril. He was midway through drying a side plate and had stopped with the dish and dish towel still in his hands. Avril continued to wash but she was smiling too.

'I've missed you too.'

'How about we get married?' Davy blurted.

Avril stopped and looked at him. 'What?'

'I mean we already have the kid.' Davy chuckled. "I know its sudden but I've always loved you and since we got back in touch it's all I've thought about.'

Avril was standing now staring at him.

'No, Davy.' Avril answered ' I can't marry you.'

Davy's face fell.

'Well, at least until you get down on one knee and ask me properly.' She laughed. Davy immediately dropped to his knee and in the loudest voice possible said.

' Avril McKay, will you marry me?'

There was an immediate clamouring from the living room as first Sophie then Maybeth followed by Nate, Jess and Ronnie came into the kitchen.

Laughing hard, Avril had her hand over her mouth.

'You better say yes, Mum.' Sophie chided

'Do it! Do it!" Jess, Nate and Maybeth chanted.

'Will you hurry up and answer me woman,' Davy grumbled 'these old joints are beginning to seize and before to long I'll be stuck down here.

'Yes, I will.' Avril said.

They all cheered and congratulated the couple. Maybeth stood with tears in her eyes. Her birth parents were back together. She was the happiest she had every felt. Ronnie came and stood beside her.

'You did this,' he said proudly. Sophie had started to organize the wedding. She had declared herself, Maybeth and Jess as bridesmaids, Nate would be the photographer.

'Can we get a ring first, Soph?' Avril laughed. 'Just let me get used to it first please.'

Davy laughed. ' Take all the time you need, I'm going nowhere.'

They chatted about letting Debbie know his evening and Avril said that Davy and she would work out the living arrangements in the New Year. She would be moving back here she knew. Just as they were getting ready to leave Nate spoke.

'Jess and I really want to thank you for a lovely day. We're so glad you're getting married Mum, we're so happy you found us all Maybeth and for the past three months we've been healing from the loss of our baby, but time moves on and two days ago we discovered that Jess is pregnant again. It's early days but this baby has actually made it into the womb this time so depending on when you set the date for your wedding Mum, Jess is going to need a HUGE dress.'

Everyone burst out laughing and once again tears and cheers were shouted. Davy left his car and he and Avril walked down to the café to see Debbie. Sophie left with Nate and Jess which left Maybeth and Ronnie alone in the house.

'What a day.' Ronnie exclaimed 'I think I need a lie down.'

'Me too.' said Maybeth. They tidied up a bit and locked the doors. Ronnie shouted from the top of the stairs, 'goodnight love.' Maybeth took a glass of water and walked upstairs. She yawned as she went. As she washed and cleaned her teeth, she replayed the days events over in her head. Taking off her clothes and pulling on her nightie she then climbed under her duvet and grinned. Today had been the best day ever. All her stars had aligned, and she felt very, very happy. Then she felt nothing, as the sleep she so badly needed suddenly and pleasantly enveloped her.